IN THE NAME OF SILENCE

M. LEE PRESCOTT

Published by Mount Hope Press

*For Abigail, Ava, Benjamin and Teddy
and joy that is boundless and seldom silent!*

CHAPTER 1

Her fiancé nuzzled her neck, sending shivers down her spine. "Have I told you I love you today?"

Bess laughed, turning to gaze into his light blue eyes, his tawny brown hair, tousled from sleep. Her hand came to rest on his chiseled chin and she marveled, as she always did, at how lucky she was to have found her beloved Harry. "About two dozen times."

"Must be slipping."

"Thank you for making the last year so happy, Mr. Winthrop."

Harry noted that she didn't say "the happiest of my life." Too much to hope with the shadow of her deceased husband always hanging over them. No matter. She loved him. They were together. It was enough. She looked especially lovely this morning in her favorite sweater, soft green cashmere. In deference to her role as weekend coordinator, she had added a jaunty scarf around her slender neck, the pattern of blues and greens a perfect complement. Hers was a soft beauty, which somehow defied description, but was deeply moving.

Harry Winthrop had loved the Widow Dore, as the villagers called her, from the moment he had laid eyes on her at a school social event. Thanks to the school's patron, dear old dad, Harry had been called to Old Harbor Friends to investigate the murder of the school's comptroller. A prime suspect at the start of the investigation, the shy and grieving widow had touched his heart in a way no other woman ever had. He vowed from their first encounter that he would prove her innocence, and more importantly, that it would be he who finally brought her out of a decade of mourning. To his delight, Harry Winthrop had succeeded and healed his own tattered heart in the process. "Are you heading into town, my love?"

"Someone has to organize the arriving guests."

"I thought Cathy and Lois were doing it? After all, the B&B is full and it's not even leaf peeper season."

"Have you forgotten that these people are Anne Greyson devotees? If they cannot be greeted by Anne herself, then it should be someone who knows Anne intimately."

"Intimately, I like the sound of that." He bent to kiss her.

"When are you planning to deliver the news about Anne's true identity?"

"I'm not. Didn't I tell you? I'm introducing *you* as Anne Greyson."

"Oh, no, you don't! I'm not playing you."

"Why not? You know the books as well as I do."

"That's not the point. It's dishonest. *You* are Anne Greyson. You're the author, not me. They've come to see *you,* not a devoted fan posing as you."

"If we do that, it'll be all over social media that the wildly successful female mystery writer, Anne Greyson, is really a boring middle-aged man."

"Can't be helped, now shoo, if you want a run! We need you in town in an hour."

The couple exchanged a long, deep kiss before Harry headed off for a jog in the woods. Bess stepped back into the cottage to collect her bag before heading into the village. In a little over a month, she would be Mrs. Winthrop and by the following summer, they would move from the cottage to the home Harry was planning on the rolling hills not far from his father's estate. Breathtaking, the turn her life had taken since Harry Winthrop walked into it.

CHAPTER 2

Roger Demaris, Head of the Regional Homicide Division (R.H.D.), sat at his desk staring at the invitation. *Bess Dore and Harry Winthrop request the pleasure of your company at their nuptials on December 15th.* The ache in his chest radiated out to his shoulders and arms until he wondered if it were the start of a heart attack. His first heart attack six months earlier had changed his life. Exercise was now a daily ritual. Between yoga, meditation, and long walks, he was a changed man, the legendary, ferocious anger gone, replaced by a steely calm that astounded those who knew him. When Mary, his ex-wife, had visited to collect some of her things, she had barely recognized him.

"You're not goin' to that, are you?"

Pete Dugan, his second in command, had stepped in and was now peering over his shoulder.

"Why not?" He shot up his hand. "Never mind, don't answer that. What's the news this morning?"

"Quiet." Dugan stared at his boss, ever watchful and fiercely protective. He had not been around when the older man had dated Bess Guilford in high school, but he had observed them together on enough occasions to know that Roger Demaris was still in love with the pleasant, but plain, art teacher. The kind of love that could destroy him. The day the engagement had been announced, Pete had actually feared for his boss' sanity.

"Well, good. Let's catch up on this mountain of paperwork, then."

Little did the two suspect that in less than an hour, the quiet would be a dim memory when news came of a terrible crime that would shatter the peaceful serenity of the village of Old Harbor forever.

CHAPTER 3

The earthy scents of bittersweet and damp fallen leaves surrounded him as Harry headed into the woods. A bobolink called from a nearby field, answered by the heckling mimicking of a mockingbird. How should he handle the Anne Greyson revelation? Bess was right. It wasn't fair to keep it a secret, but the anonymity had been comforting.

He loved the woodland paths surrounding the cottage and the school campus of Old Harbor Friends. After skirting the campus, he had plunged into woods. The path, if followed to its conclusion, led to the vast Winthrop lands, hundreds of acres to the south. His footsteps were muffled on the soft dirt path. As he picked up his pace, he ran through fingers of light playing through the dense forest. His last thought as he entered a clearing, to the left of which was a labyrinth constructed by students, was that he was the luckiest man alive. He would soon marry the love of his life. He had never been happier.

Barely had those thoughts crossed his mind, as they did dozens of times each day, when the arrow pierced his chest and Harry fell to the soft earthen floor, all thought obliterated forever.

CHAPTER 4

Cathy Nolan, owner of the Honeysuckle B&B, threw up her hands and gave Bess an exasperated look. "Where should we put the Stewarts at dinner tonight? They're at the inn. Did you meet them at the Reception? It's a couple, I think, but they didn't say. Could be siblings, cousins? Names are John and June."

"Let's wait and see. I say we assign tables after lunch. I'll make a point to stop in at the inn and try to put names to faces, or ask whoever is at the front desk."

The two had been working all morning, making place cards, stuffing folders, planning menus, and checking and rechecking reservations. There were twenty people registered for the weekend, half of who were staying at the B&B, the others at the inn three doors away. With the exception of one of Harry's publishers, all who had arrived the previous evening. Liz Reynolds, his assistant of many years, had come for the Reception, then returned to Boston, but was expected back shortly to stay for the weekend.

"Where's your hubby-to-be, anyway? Didn't you expect him hours ago?"

"Yes, and I've been trying to phone him. My guess is that he met someone on his run and is now distracted in conversation or helping with some job or other."

"Always was a do-gooder, your Harry. How about we break for lunch and maybe he'll show up at the Tavern wanting to satisfy that enormous appetite of his."

"Good idea," she said, setting down a pile of pocket folders and grabbing the large woven backpack that served as purse and general catch all.

They strolled across Main Street to Tilly's Tavern, owned by a couple who made the best sandwiches and salads in the village. Tilly cooked and Rachel managed the popular spot where lunch and dinner were served seven days a week. Occasionally they prepared sumptuous brunches, but they refrained from offering daily breakfast so as not to compete with the bakery and Café on Main Street.

Bess ordered a BLT with Tilly's special sauce and kale chips. Cathy ordered a Gorgonzola burger and sweet potato curly fries. They both asked for Tilly's tea, a sweet lemony iced tea with secret ingredients that Tilly refused to divulge.

When their lunches arrived, the pair ate in silence for a few minutes, then chatted about the weekend's events, wondering again what had happened to the absent-minded Harry, aka Anne Greyson, star of the weekend. As they sipped the last of their tea, sated and ready to pay and head back to the B&B, the Tavern door swung open.

CHAPTER 5

"Sir, we've got a situation."

Ashen-faced, Dugan stood in his superior's doorway. It was never a good sign when Pete called him "sir."

Demaris gazed up from the sports page up, astounded by his assistant's pallor. He had the impulse to run, to avoid hearing news that somehow he knew would hit close to home. Instead, he set the newspaper aside and sat up. "What's up?"

"It's Harry Winthrop."

"The elder?"

"No, the son."

"What's he, amateur sleuthing again? I thought this was his big mystery weekend." In addition to the city paper, Demaris never failed to read the weekly *Old Harbor Gazette.*

"He's dead, Rodge."

"Dead? Where? How?"

"Murdered."

"What?"

"They found him in the woods near the school playing fields."

"Jesus Christ! What happened?"

"Someone shot him with a bow and arrow."

Demaris stared at the younger man for several minutes, stunned.

"Sir, we should get going."

"Who found him?"

"Don't know. They didn't say. Guess we'll find out when we get there."

"Local cops?"

"On the scene, but they've called for you. Want me to get the car?"

"You and Greta head over there with the team. Keep the local guys back so they don't trample over everything. See where Megan is, too."

"What about you?"

"I'll be there as soon as I can. There's a notification. Does she know?"

"Far as I know, no one knows except local cops."

"The old man?"

"Dunno. Aren't you coming with us?"

"No, I'll be there as soon as I can, but I'm going through town first."

"But—"

For an instant, the familiar fire flashed in Demaris' eyes, but just as quickly it vanished and when he spoke, his voice was calm. "You and Greta are perfectly capable of securing a crime scene. Now get going. Call if there's anything I should know." He gave his assistant a grim smile. "It's okay, Mother Hen. I'll join you soon as I can."

As he drove the fifteen miles from his new office at R.H.D., Demaris reflected on the strange turns his life had taken over the past decades. A tour in Iraq, a marriage that exploded after five years, and now a job he enjoyed, except on days like this one.

He and Mary had never had a chance. Mary knew he loved Bess Guilford when they married. She had been around to observe devastating effects of their high school break-up on Roger Demaris. Then he disappeared overseas. When he got out of the service, Mary thought she could win his heart. When she had not succeeded, she hoped the birth of their daughter Theresa, now almost ten, might finally obliterate his feelings for his high school sweetheart. Nothing had worked. After five lonely years, Mary had had enough and moved to Ohio to be near family, taking his precious Terry with her. He barely saw his daughter, maybe once or twice a year. Occasionally, Mary brought her for a visit or he traveled to Ohio, where he never felt welcome. What a mess he had made of it all.

"The heart wants what the heart wants," the therapist had told him. "Grieve and go on. She's happy now with yet another man. Time to let go. Open yourself up to other possibilities."

Letting go was easier said than done. How does one let go of feelings that reside in the depth of one's soul? He was happy for Bess. He had even developed a grudging respect for her carefree, flamboyant fiancé, who clearly made her happy. But, let go? Impossible.

He called the Honeysuckle B&B and was told that Bess was lunching at the Tavern with Cathy. He then called Jane Fellows, Bess' dear friend and colleague, and asked her to meet him outside the Tavern. When he pulled up and parked, Jane was waiting. Taking a deep breath, he stepped from the car, heart heavy, dreading the terrible task ahead.

"Ready?"

She nodded and they headed in.

CHAPTER 6

Even though the day was warm, a chill crept over Bess as she turned toward the door. Framed in the sunlight, she spied not her fiancé, but Roger. Beside him stood an unlikely companion, her dear friend, Jane. Their faces grave, Bess simultaneously understood that they had come together and that they brought terrible news. He looked tired, jacket rumpled, thick hair tousled as if he had just climbed out of bed. Even in her fear, she noticed that the jacket was part of a suit, an expensive one that appeared to have been tailored to fit his short, broad-shouldered frame. He had lost weight and his thick, chestnut hair was longer than she remembered.

Sad, dark eyes held hers as the pair came nearer. Jane came forward first and pulled up a chair beside her, arm circling her shoulders.

She began to tremble and her eyes darted from Jane to her companion. "What is it? What's happened?"

Demaris pulled up a chair and positioned himself directly in front of her. He reached forward and took her hands in his. "There's been an accident."

"Oh, God, something's happened to Harry. Has he been in a car crash? Is he at the hospital? What's happened?"

"Bess, I'm so sorry to have to tell you, but Harry's dead."

"Dead? Jane?"

"I'm so sorry, sweetheart."

Jane Fellows reached around and tried to fold her friend in her arms, but Bess sprung to her feet and flailed her arms, eyes wild and unseeing. "No, no, it's not true! I just saw him. He went for a run. It must be someone else!"

Demaris stood and tried to grab hold of her, but she struck out and pounded his chest and shoulders as she screamed and sobbed. All eyes in the crowded restaurant followed every nuance of the heartbreaking scene. Finally, he succeeded in grabbing hold of her, clasping her tightly in his arms to tame the wild gesturing. He motioned to Cathy. "You and Jane take her back to the B & B where it's quiet. Get her a brandy. I've got to get out there."

"Out where?"

"The woods behind campus. Pete's with him."

"I'm coming."

"No, you're not. Jane and Cathy'll take care of you. I'll come back as soon as I can."

"Roger, I'm coming!"

He took hold of her shoulders and the dark blue eyes bore into hers. "No, Bess, I cannot let you and I know Harry wouldn't want you to be there. I promise, I'll come back soon."

He transferred her to Cathy and Jane's arms, one on either side. Then, he retreated lest she follow and see what no fiancée should see, her betrothed with an arrow protruding from his chest. Jesus Christ, what kind of sick son of a bitch does something like this?

As Demaris stepped out of the Tavern, a tall, buxom blonde passed him, and he heard her throaty voice speak to the group he had just left behind.

"Hey, guys, is Harry around? I barely saw him last night. Where is he?"

"Jesus Christ," he muttered as Bess' strangled screams sounded behind him. His instinct was to turn and go back to take her in his arms, but he pressed onward. Whoever the newcomer was, he predicted she would be screaming next.

CHAPTER 7

A grim tableau greeted him as he reached the clearing. He glanced at the string of tattered Tibetan prayer flags fluttering to his left as he neared the group standing in a spot about two hundred yards from the Old Harbor Friends soccer field. Pete and Greta were circling the body, the latter snapping photos, the former seemingly lost in thought. R.H.D's forensic pathologist, Megan Kreiger had arrived and was crouched over the body, gingerly examining the arrow that protruded from Harry Winthrop's chest.

New to the team, Megan replaced the elderly physician who had refused to work with Demaris. She had requested a transfer from Pennsylvania to follow her fiancé, Derek, who was completing his pediatric residency at Hasbro in Providence, Rhode Island. She was thrilled to be working with R.H.D. and its dark, brooding head.

"So, what've we got, Meg?"

"Well, cause of death is obvious. Probably didn't know what hit him, poor guy. I'd say he's been gone about three or four hours. I'll know more when we get him on the table. Have we got a lab?"

"County's lending us a space at the Clinic," Dugan said, directing his remarks at his boss. "Meg's equipment should be there in an hour."

"Good work."

Dugan regarded his boss, concern in his pale blue eyes. "Did you see her?"

"If you mean Ms. Dore, yes, she's been notified."

"How is she?"

Demaris ignored the question. "Any chance this was an accident?"

"Not likely," Dugan replied.

"Any idea where the shooter was standing?"

One of the three local police officers stepped forward. "Sir, it looks like he or she was lying in wait behind that stand of hemlock, near the maze."

"It's a labyrinth," he said, turning to smile at the officer who appeared no older than fifteen. His uniform looked shiny and new, and short brown hair peeked out from under a stiff O.H.P.D. baseball cap. "Thank you, Officer?"

"Brendan, sir, I mean, Officer Brendan Stevens."

Demaris turned to his second-in-command. "Pete, did you check that out with Officer Stevens?"

Dugan nodded. "Ground tamped down, bushes parted. Looks like that could have been the spot, especially in relation to how the body fell."

"Show me."

After a brief inspection of the spot in question, the three men returned to the clearing. Demaris stooped on one knee to examine the still figure. His demeanor registered sadness. Death brought a terrible weight that pressed on one's chest making each breath labored. Who the hell would want to kill the most popular guy in the village? It didn't make any sense.

"Okay, as soon as Meg's through, let's get the poor bastard out of here. Pete and Greta, take a couple of these guys with you and go back into town. We'll need to talk to all the out-of-towners here for the weekend. No one leaves, understand?"

Dugan nodded. "What about the locals?"

"Same thing. No one leaves this village until we say so. Jesus Christ, I wonder if anyone's told the old man. I'll head back to the B&B and check in with them."

"I can do that, sir."

Dugan knew he was overstepping, but the look on his boss' face when he talked about "checking in" was a dead giveaway. What he meant was, "I'll check in with her."

"Didn't I just give you plenty to do?"

"Yes, sir, of course. Let's go, guys."

Dugan turned away. He would get a reprimand later, no doubt about it.

Greta Burke, new to the team, watched the interchange from the sidelines. Their technology wiz, Greta was also a careful, observant investigator. In her two months with R.H.D., she had participated in two homicide investigations, but had never witnessed this kind of interaction between Dugan and his superior. What was going on? That the two men were very close had been obvious from day one. There was often playful banter and kidding between them, but also respect. She had never seen Pete be insubordinate.

Demaris smiled at the young woman, her flaxen, shoulder-length hair uncombed as usual, jeans stained, jacket wrinkled. Greta always looked as if they had dragged her out of bed. Normally, he might have made a suggestion for her to pull herself together, but instead he turned away and ignored Dugan completely. He needed to get to Harry Winthrop Senior before someone else did.

"Greta, we're going to need a space. See what you can find and I'll ask in town as well."

CHAPTER 8

When Demaris reached the B&B, the front hall and parlor were filled with people, none of whom he recognized except Lois Arnold, one of the owners. Neither her partner, Cathy Nolan, nor Bess were in the front rooms. Lois appeared to be mingling, passing drinks and tiny sandwiches. When she spotted him, she set down her tray and snaked through the throng to his side.

"Why, if it isn't our former constable come home. How's life with the big guys treating you?"

Demaris smiled at the short, dark-haired innkeeper, genuinely glad to see her. "She came from sturdy stock" might be how one would describe Lois. Not heavy, but solid. Her brown hair was tied back in a long, thick braid, her charcoal eyes alert and watchful. She was dressed in jeans and a man's plaid flannel shirt covered with a slightly soiled denim apron, *Honeysuckle B&B* emblazoned across the breast pocket in lavender script.

Lois held out her arms and he returned her embrace. "Hello, Lo, good to see you. You're looking well."

"Still a bullshitter, I see. Terrible, isn't it? Poor, poor Bess. I'm not sure she can survive this without going crazy. It's just been this past year that she's pulled out of her turtle shell. I mean, we all loved Mac, but ten years is enough already."

"Where is she?"

"In the kitchen with Cath and Jane. Thought it best to keep her away from the weekend crowd. They all know about Harry, by the way, and are completely freaked out. They wanted to pack their bags and hightail it, so they are none too happy now that Pete and his very attractive partner have informed them that they have to stay indefinitely. You're lucky they haven't seen you or there might be a second murder."

"Where're Pete and Greta now?"

"Headed for the inn. Most from the readers' group are here, but there are five or six who went back to their rooms for a nap. Maybe a couple at the Tavern for a drink?"

"I've got an errand to run, then the team will come back to talk with them. Did Greta ask about a space for us to set up?"

"Yes, and I suggested the guest house behind the Tavern. Tilly and Rach rent it by the week and month and there's no one there now. Two rooms, bathroom, small kitchen."

"Perfect, thanks. I'm close enough to go home, but one or more of them might want to stay in the village. Any rooms available?"

"Inn's full and we are, too, but if you get stuck, you can use a couple of our rooms. Cath and I keep two for our guests and they're empty now."

"Thanks, Lo. I'll pop my head in the kitchen, then check back later. You keeping her here?"

"Keeps saying she wants to go home. I think Jane was going to go with her."

He nodded and turned away, eyes sad, expression grim. What he would find in the kitchen would break his heart. He took a deep breath and pushed the swinging door.

Bess sat at the table with Jane and Cathy. The three looked up as he entered and Bess rose. Jane Fellows was a striking woman with long thick red hair, not a hint of gray, Her deep green eyes registered concern as she tried, unsuccessfully, to keep her friend seated. Although in her mid-forties, Jane could pass for ten years younger. Today, she was dressed in what appeared to be black yoga pants and a flowing, long- sleeved tunic in a deep purple shade that flattered her curvaceous figure. Enormous silver-hooped earrings dangled from her ears. Beside her, Bess looked plain, almost dowdy, in sensible khaki slacks and a pale green sweater, a rumpled scarf her only adornment.

Blue-green eyes, wild with grief, stared up at him. "Did you see him?"

He nodded, opened his arms and she collapsed against him sobbing. After several minutes he eased her back to her chair and knelt beside her. "Why don't you let Jane take you home."

Incoherent and trembling, she shook her head. Jane's arm caressed her shoulders as Bess patted tears away with a soggy linen napkin monogrammed *H&B*.

"Two glasses of brandy," Cathy said quietly. "Should I get another?"

He looked from Jane to Cathy and wondered why they were asking him for advice. Clearly all three were in shock. Any lifeline would do.

"Call Doc Collins. Have him meet you at the cottage, if he's free. If not, ask him to give her something to help her sleep."

As Cathy reached for her cell phone and retreated to a corner to make the call, he turned to the others. "I'm going out to the hall to see his dad. Has she spoken to him?"

"Oh, my God," Bess wailed. "Why didn't I think of Mr. Winthrop? This will kill him!"

He took hold of her hands and settled them in her lap. "He's tough."

"I'm coming with you."

"No, you're not. You stay with Jane and Cathy. They'll get something from the doc to help you rest."

"Don't be ridiculous. He was about to be my father-in-law. He should hear the news from me."

"That's not a good idea, Bess," he said softly, still holding her hands. "I know he'll want to see you, but not like this. You need to rest and collect yourself. I'll stop back later and let you know how things go. Okay?"

She turned away and buried her face against Jane's shoulder.

CHAPTER 9

With a nod to the other women, he pushed open the door, nearly colliding with a tall, broad-shouldered man, who bore a remarkable resemblance to Harry Winthrop. Although dark-haired with intense brown eyes, he held himself with the robust confidence of the privileged. He wondered if the preppy stranger had been listening at the keyhole.

"Detective?"

"Yes?" he replied, looking up at the man who towered over him.

"I apologize, I was eavesdropping. I had started to follow you into the kitchen until I heard poor Ms. Dore's cries and thought I'd better wait out here."

"And, you are?"

"Tim Hargreaves, Harry's friend."

"Are you a local person, Mr. Hargreaves?"

He laughed. "Hardly. I'm from New York, but I live in Greenleaf now. Teach at the college." He referred to a New England college town about forty-five minutes north of Old Harbor. "Greenleaf's quiet, but this place makes Greenleaf look like Times Square."

"Were you enrolled in the Anne Greyson weekend?"

"Yup. Harry and I thought it'd be a hoot to have me come. I'm not a mystery reader, but it would've given us a chance to catch up. I've been on sabbatical this past year and traveling abroad so I'd never met the fiancée either."

"And have you?"

"Excuse me?"

"Met Ms. Dore?"

"Only briefly last night when I checked in. She was busy so Harry and I went over and grabbed a bite in the taproom. She joined us for soup at the tail end."

"I see. How did you know Harry?"

"We go way back. We were roommates at Exeter. He's my main man when it comes to travel. We've been all over the world together."

Demaris wondered if Hargreaves fancied himself to be a character in a British sitcom. Main man, indeed. Dressed in jeans, running shoes, and a Greenleaf College sweatshirt, his good looks had attracted the notice of most of the women, several of whom stared unabashedly.

"I wonder if you might step out the front door with me, Mr. Hargreaves?"

"Of course."

Once outside, Demaris pulled out his small notebook and pen. "Now, perhaps you can tell me why you were eavesdropping? Do you have information about Mr. Winthrop's death?"

Hargreaves looked stricken. "Of course not! I'm devastated about Harry, just like everyone else. No, I wanted to see if I could help. Maybe take Bess home, offer comfort. I was also thinking of the old man. Harry Senior and I go way back. Would you like me to go with you? Might soften the blow to have a friend present?"

"That's very kind of you, but it will be most helpful if you remain here and available to my detectives. Are you staying here or at the inn?"

"Inn, but Lo, Cath, and I are already old friends."

"I see. Is this your first visit to Old Harbor?"

"Yup. Harry and I usually meet in Boston."

"So you know about his penname?"

"Know? I was with him when he dreamed it up. We were trekking in Nepal when he was plotting the first book. Suddenly, one morning he said, 'Anne Greyson, what'dya think?' And I said, 'yuck, dullsville,' but, Harry never listens to anyone. Did you know him, Detective?"

Ignoring the man's question and the second slight to his rank, of which Demaris was certain Hargreaves was aware, he said, "And did you have an idea?"

"I suggested Lola La Lane, or something like that. Something that said sexy and alluring."

"I've never read the books, but my understanding is that they fall into the cozy genre, not sexy romance."

"Who cares? It's all about selling books, mate! Let 'em discover the boring, cozy stuff after they've bought the book."

Biting back a sarcastic remark about the man's ridiculous imitation of an Aussie sitcom actor, Demaris made a mental note to pick up copies of all Anne Greyson books. Time to read about what might have gotten the poor bastard killed.

"Do you have anything to add at this time, Mr. Hargreaves? What were you up to this morning, for example?"

"I slept in, stopped here to grab one of Cath's incredible cranberry muffins, and headed out for a hike."

"Oh?"

"In the opposite direction from where I understand they found Harry. I took one of the mountain trails on the map Lois gave me. Went as far as the lake, then came back just as the news broke."

"Anyone with you?"

"No, trail and village deserted. Tried to interest a couple of my fellow workshop members in coming along. Asked that bumptious ass, Stewart, and his bubblehead girlfriend, but they were going jogging on the school track. Could anything be more boring?"

"Yes, well, thank you, Mr. Hargreaves. We'll be in touch to take your formal statement later on. If you think of anything in the meantime, give me or one of my detectives a call. Numbers are all here." He handed him a card and turned away.

"Oh, it's Lieutenant Demaris. Please forgive my mistake!"

CHAPTER 10

Winthrop Hall, the nickname the locals had given it, stood at the crest of a hill looking westward over the village of Old Harbor. A half-mile road led to the circular driveway and the front entrance to the Victorian mansion. Its clapboards and lacy gingerbread always appeared as if they'd been given a fresh coat of white paint. Behind the house, the lawn gave way gradually to fields of wildflowers bordered with stonewalls that stretched eastward toward the sea. Garages and several outbuildings dotted the property, all tucked away in inconspicuous locations so as not to spoil the view.

As he stepped from the car, he regretted that he had not brought Pete or Greta with him. There were several cars in the driveway in addition to his dark, green jeep. No sooner had he knocked than the housekeeper, Helen Stevens, swung open the door.

"Hello, Lieutenant, we've been expecting you."

"Excuse me?"

"My nephew, Brendan, just phoned to say you were on your way, but Mr. Winthrop has been waiting for over three hours."

He followed the tall, gray-haired woman with ramrod straight in straight charcoal gray wool skirt, and matching sweater. Her sensible, rubber-soled shoes moved soundlessly across the foyer's marble floor. She opened the door to the study where he found Harry Winthrop Senior engaged in conversation with two men, neither of whom were familiar to Demaris.

"Demaris, thank you for coming."

"I take it my appearance is not a surprise, sir?"

"These are my attorneys, Lester Franklin and Richard D'Angelis. They were just leaving."

The two men, dark suits and similar wiry countenances, could have passed for brothers. On closer inspection, Franklin appeared to be considerably older than his companion. He stepped forward and grasped Roger's hand in a firm handshake.

"Pleasure to meet you, sir. Unfortunately under such terrible circumstances."

Demaris nodded and moved to shake D'Angelis' hand. Grasp not so firm, eyes down, a nod his only greeting.

Harry Winthrop waved his hand in dismissal. "They're from Boston. Gentlemen, thank you. Les, I'll be in touch. Thank you for coming."

Taking their cue, the two stood and departed quickly.

"Please, sit, Lieutenant."

He took a seat in the armchair to the right of where Winthrop sat in a deep, chestnut leather armchair. "Roger, please."

"Can I get you something to drink? Pierce!" he called and Molly Pierce, the cook, poked her head in another door at the opposite end of the room.

"No, thank you, sir. I'm fine."

She closed the door without a word.

Demaris cleared his throat and turned to his host. "Then you know about your son?"

"Who do you think had you called in?"

"You?"

"I still have a few friends in high places. I wouldn't trust the local constabulary to investigate the inside of a chicken coop. Chief Wilbur is away, but as you well know, the man's an incompetent buffoon."

Silently agreeing with the assessment of his former boss, Demaris asked, "How did you learn about Harry?"

"Someone called and told Pierce, then hung up immediately. I sent Ralph out to the woods and he found him. Ralph called me and I phoned Senator Rogers."

Demaris studied the frail octogenarian, who despite his efficient recitation of the morning's events, was shaken to his core and appeared ready to keel over. His hands shook violently whenever he raised them from his lap and his eyes were red-rimmed.

"I'm so sorry about your son. He was a remarkable person."

Winthrop started to speak, but tears welled in his eyes and he fell silent instead, staring at the floor. When he finally spoke, his voice was barely a whisper. "Find the monster who did this. Please."

"We will. Do you have someone to stay with you?"

"My son was the last of my family. There is no one. But Molly, Helen, and Ralph will be with me."

"I'd like to speak with Molly. Then with Ralph, if I may?"

Winthrop nodded. "She'll be in the kitchen, or in her rooms, behind the pantry. Ralph's probably in the back gardens. Shall I ring for them?"

"I'll find them."

"Thank you for coming so quickly."

Demaris nodded, eyes solemn as he regarded the grief-stricken father. "Can you think of anyone who would want to harm Harry?"

"I've thought of nothing else since Ralph's call. Everyone loved my son, Lieutenant. He had no enemies."

Everyone has enemies, Demaris thought. He stood and smiled down at his host. "I'll be off then. If you hear anything, we are setting up at the guest house behind the Tavern." He placed a card on the table beside him. "My numbers and Detectives Dugan's and Burke's are there. You know Pete, and Greta Burke is very competent. If anything comes up day or night, please do not hesitate to call any of us."

As he turned away, a gnarled, shaking hand grasped his arm. "You will keep me informed, won't you?"

Demaris placed his hand gently over the other's. "Of course. Try to get some rest."

"Lieutenant, there's something different about you. A calm, or quiet. Is it the title or might pharmaceuticals be involved?"

Despite the gravity of the situation, Demaris chuckled. "No drugs and it certainly isn't the title. It's a longer conversation for another day. Let's just say, I let go of a lifetime of anger and leave it at that."

"Yes, another day," Winthrop replied, withdrawing a quivering hand and placing it under his other. "I truly am interested."

CHAPTER 11

Demaris found Molly Pierce in the back garden picking lettuces and herbs. When she spied him she looked stricken. He sat on a stone bench at the edge of the garden.

"I'm so sorry for your loss. Might I have a short word, Ms. Pierce?" He patted the bench, hoping she would join him, which she did, setting down her basket down beside her with trembling hands.

"It's Molly, sir."

"Do you remember me?"

She nodded. "You used to be a village constable."

He smiled, regarding her with kind eyes. "Something like that. I was a detective here in Old Harbor for a number of years, but I work for the state now, in a special homicide division. I gather Mr. Winthrop called for us?"

She nodded and stared at the dirt path in front of them.

"Molly, do you know anyone who might want to hurt Harry?"

She shook her head and tears spilled over to run down her cheeks. He pulled out a clean handkerchief and placed it in her lap.

"No," she wailed, a fresh spate of tears commencing. Finally, she dried her eyes and began wringing his handkerchief with mud-stained hands. "Everyone loved Mr. Harry. Why would anyone want to hurt him?"

"Mr. Winthrop tells me you answered the phone this morning. Did you recognize the caller's voice?"

She shook her head.

"Man or woman?"

"It's hard to say. He or she muffled her voice. It was deep, but I suppose it could be either."

"What did he or she say?"

"Harry Winthrop has finally gotten what he deserves. See for yourself in the West Woods."

"Then what?"

"I asked who was calling, but the phone went dead."

"Then what did you do?"

"Well, I hated to do it, but I woke Mr. Winthrop. He usually sleeps until ten or eleven. He asked me to fetch Ralph and have him take the truck to West Woods immediately. I found Ralph in the barn and he headed right out."

"What time was this?"

"I'd say around nine, but I can't be sure."

"The caller didn't ring again?"

His handkerchief was now a tattered mess. Molly shook her head. He sat silent beside the grief- stricken cook for several minutes until her sobs subsided. "Can I get you a glass of water?"

"No, thank you, sir. I'll go in now."

He reached into his pocket and extracted his card. "If you think of anything else, please give us a call, day or night."

She nodded and he headed off in the direction of the barn to find Ralph Boardman.

Chapter 12

He found the gardener in the barn loading a wheelbarrow with various tools. Life going on, despite the horrific events of the morning. Boardman turned and as he approached, he tipped a soiled, rumpled baseball hat. Dressed in worn jeans and a moth-eaten red flannel shirt, thick leather gloves protruded from his pockets. His work boots appeared to have been recently repaired with duct tape.

"So, you're back?"

"It would appear so, yes. I'm surprised to find you back at work so soon after—"

"After finding young Mr. Harry? What else is there to do? If the old man wants to go into town, I want to be close by so I can take him."

"For what reason?"

"Said he wanted to see Mrs. Dore."

"I would suggest that you, Helen, and Molly try to keep him here. I imagine Mrs. Dore will come to see him as soon as she's able."

"'I expect so."

"Anything you can tell me about this morning?"

"Molly came and told me Mr. Winthrop wanted me to go out to West Woods to look for Harry so I headed right out. Didn't take long to find him. Wasn't too far in."

Demaris nodded. "Anything you noticed when you arrived?"

"You mean aside from Mr. Harry with an arrow sticking out of his chest? Not really. Was quiet. Good thing, too, 'cause that's a popular jogging route with the kids."

"Oh? And, you know this because?"

Boardman gave him a sharp look and sat silent for a few seconds before replying. "I walk there. In the mornings and sometimes early evenings. It's not far and doc says I need to walk. According to him, manual labor is not enough to keep me healthy."

"Was anyone else around?"

"Just as I was parking the truck, a jogger came by. Hard to tell if he or she had come from that path or one of the others. Hood up, never saw the face. Had a bulky jacket so could have been girl or boy."

"What else did you notice about this person?"

"About five ten, maybe six feet, thin, navy pants, and matching jacket, one of those jogging suits they all wear. Hooded sweatshirt was underneath, could've been a school shirt. Gray, I think it was."

"Did you notice hair color, shoes?"

"Nope. Sorry. I was so eager to get to Mr. Harry. I was hoping he'd still be alive so I'm 'fraid I didn't pay much attention."

To someone who could have been the killer, Demaris mused, reaching into his back pocket and handing the man his card. "Please call day or night, if you think of anything. We're setting up a space in town, probably the Tavern's guest house. Please try to have Mr. Winthrop stay put."

"We'll try, but he's stubborn."

"So sorry for your loss."

Sadness shone in Boardman's eyes. "Thanks. This is gonna kill him, you know."

CHAPTER 13

As he turned onto the village's main street, Demaris called Pete's cell to get an update.

"I'm at the inn, boss. Some of the weekend people are screamin' to leave. It's kind of a madhouse."

"Have Greta or Stevens get the phone records for Winthrop Hall ASAP. The bastard called somewhere between eight and nine."

"Will do."

Demaris clicked off and parked two blocks from the Harbor Inn. What he really wanted to do was head for the cottage in the woods at the edge of campus, but Jane was with her. His job was here.

Bedlam reigned in the inn's double parlors, which served as lobby and lounge areas for guests. Pete stood near the desk talking to the same striking blonde he had passed earlier on his way out of the Tavern. Behind them, a couple stood, the man waving his hands, vainly endeavoring to get anyone's attention. When he spied his boss, Pete waved and gestured for the couple to wait as he broke free of the blonde.

"Hey, boss, glad you're here." Red-faced, Pete's eyes wildly scanned the room, waiting for the next assault.

"Where's Greta?"

"Greta's over at the guest house setting things up. Stevens stayed with Meg in the woods. Local guys, too. "

"Call her, then get everyone involved in the Anne Greyson weekend here. I'd like to speak with them all together. Have you got a list?"

Dugan took a folded paper from his pocket. "Got it from Lois at the B&B."

"Well grab the others and get everyone assembled in an hour. People can't have gone far. Check the Tavern, B&B, and up and down Main."

"There are a few that wanna talk to you now."

"Not now, I've got something I need to check on."

"She's gone home, sir. She's probably sedated."

Pete braced himself for the explosion, but his boss said nothing for several long minutes. Finally, Demaris patted his shoulder. "Thanks, Pete. I know what I'm doing."

"Inspector! Inspector! We need to speak with you this instant."

The man who had been standing behind Pete and the blonde, now barred the door. His companion, a short, compact redhead with tight curls and a silky mauve jogging suit, hung back. They appeared to be in their forties, maybe early fifties. He was quite a bit taller than her, his jogging suit the same silky fabric in navy, with white stripes down the side. His thinning sandy hair featured an unflattering comb-over, which now stuck out at odd angles after he removed his "Weekend with Anne" baseball cap.

"Whoa, sir. Sounds like you've been watching too many British mysteries. We don't have inspectors on this side of the Atlantic. I'm Lieutenant Demaris, from the Regional Homicide Division. I assume from your hat that you're here for the mystery weekend?"

"Which has now been canceled!"

"Yes, unfortunately one of the townspeople, and organizer, has been killed."

"Anne Greyson, you mean! Not only have we been duped all these years thinking Anne was a woman, we now come to this God-forsaken wilderness to find her murdered and a man to boot!"

"How tragic for you."

"Now see here, Inspector—"

"Let me stop you, Mr.?"

"Stewart, John Stewart."

"Mr. Stewart, I understand your distress, but the situation cannot be helped. We cannot allow anyone to leave the village right now, at least not until we have interviewed them. Do you and your wife live nearby?"

"June is my companion. We come from Concord, New Hampshire. June's the one who introduced me to the Greyson books and we've both read all of them."

Demaris consulted his watch. "I see. Well, Mr. Stewart, my assistant is gathering everyone up for a meeting at three forty five. We'll try to explain things then. Perhaps you and your companion could have a coffee and relax?"

With a "humph," Stewart turned his back and headed toward the other parlor, June following in his wake. Demaris gave Pete a wry smile and headed out, leaving his assistant to herd the cats.

It was a five-minute drive to the cottage. He spied Jane Fellows' mini and pulled up beside it. As he made his way to the door, he composed his thoughts. He had just raised his hand to knock when Jane swung the door open, finger to her lips.

"I've just gotten her to lie down. Doc gave her a sedative. I think she's asleep."

"Jane! I hear you! Who is it?"

"Shoot," the redhead said, opening the door to let him pass. "In there," she said, pointing toward the study.

Bess sat up from the soft leather couch, plaid blanket cast aside. Her eyes were puffy and her normally alabaster cheeks were covered with crimson blotches. A tattered handkerchief wrung in a tight spiral sat in her lap. Her eyes beseeched him, begging to be told it wasn't true. "Roger?"

Demaris pulled a straight-backed chair to sit in front of her. "Bess, I'm so sorry."

Her body trembled and he longed to take her in his arms, but instead, he reached forward and took both her small hands in his.

Jane stood beside her friend. "Can I get you something? Tea? Coffee?"

He shook his head and looked from one to the other. "Have you phoned people? Is someone letting people at the school know?"

"Yes, Peter offered."

Jane referred to the retired headmaster, Peter Thurbert. After traveling the previous spring, Peter and his wife, Carrie, had come back to live near Old Harbor.

"What about Mrs. Guilford? Have you phoned your mother?"

Bess shook her head.

"Would you like Jane or me to do it?"

"She's flying in tomorrow. She and her husband, Tim, were coming to the final banquet to meet Harry."

"They've never met?"

"You know Mother. She's always traveling or searching for a new husband."

"Someone should call her."

"I'll do it," Jane said quietly, patting her friend's hand.

Bess nodded and turned to him. "How's dear Mr. Winthrop?"

"About how you'd expect. The person responsible for this called him, told him where to find Harry."

"Why, Roger? Why would someone want to hurt him? He was the kindest, warmest person you'd ever want to meet."

"Yes."

"But, why?"

"We'll find him or her."

"Couldn't Mr. Winthrop tell if the caller was male or female?" Jane asked.

"It was Molly Pierce who answered. She says the voice was muffled and could have been either."

"Should I go to the Hall? Could I be helpful?"

"No, sweetheart," Jane said, arm circling Bess' shoulders.

Shrugging away from her friend's grasp, she said, "Roger, what do you think? Should I go?"

"No, you should stay right here. Lie down and try to get some rest."

She hopped up. "Lie down? Rest? How can I rest when Harry's killer is out there somewhere? Poor Mr. Winthrop, I've got to go to him. How can I lie down when an inn full of people are waiting to meet Anne Greyson? Oh, God, what will we tell them?"

"Bess, that's enough," he said, quietly. He stood and placed his hands on her shoulders. "They know. It's all taken care of. Mr. Winthrop is probably in bed, where you should be. This is what Harry would want."

She gazed into his soft eyes for several seconds, then her body crumbled. Strong arms caught her and helped her back to the couch. "Okay, there you go."

He turned to Jane. "Has she got some brandy?"

"But the pills?"

"It won't matter. Just get it."

After settling her on the couch, Roger covered Bess with the blanket and stood, allowing Jane to take the chair. He poured brandy into the glass she offered and handed it to her. "Small sips, but get it into her. Should be enough to knock her out. You staying?"

She nodded.

"I'd keep her quiet and protected from unwanted visitors." As if on cue, he spied Peter Thurbert through the window strolling up the driveway.

"Oh, Lord, just what I need. I just got rid of Tim Hargreaves and now him."

"Hargreaves was here?"

"Yes, arrived on our heels, wanting to help, moon over Bess, commiserate. Who knows. I mean, the man's gorgeous, but this was not the time. I sent him on his way as I will you know who."

"Good, I've got to get back. Thanks for taking care of her."

"Always."

She gave him a knowing smile before turning to scowl at Thurbert. Demaris was aware of their affair of many years, now over, and felt sorry for Jane. She could do better. He turned to face the newcomer.

"Good to see you again, Detective. How is she?"

Dressed casually in khakis and blue cashmere sweater, the tall, lanky Thurbert looked rested, less haunted than the last time the two had met. His salt-and-pepper hair was longer and the ends curled at the collar of a pink dress shirt.

"'Bout what you'd expect. Jane's trying to get brandy into her so she'll sleep. If you go in, don't stay long. They both need quiet."

The other man nodded, then hesitated, unsure of whether to proceed. "Terrible thing, isn't it? Have you any leads?"

"No. Don't suppose you were out jogging this morning and saw anything?"

"Bad knees. My wife Carrie's the jogger, but she usually runs on the roads so I doubt she was over that way."

"Was she out this morning?"

"Every morning, hour run from about eight to nine. When did he? I mean?"

"M.E. still determining the time, but that sounds about right. Left Bess for a run about eight."

"Oh, dear, I'll ask Carrie if she saw anything, of course."

"I'll send someone over to talk with her. Thanks."

"Poor Bess, another terrible death. This past year she had finally begun to heal after Mac."

"Yes."

"And Mr. Winthrop? Does he know?"

"He's the one who phoned us, or his friends in high places called us in."

"Poor man, so much tragedy in that family."

"Yes," Demaris said, remembering about the accident that had killed his wife and daughter, Harry's younger sister. Then there was the car crash that had taken the life of Harry's fiancée, what was her name? Sylvia? Susan?

"I've got to head out. Will you and your wife be home this evening?" Thurbert nodded. "Good, someone will come by. Remember, not too long in there."

He watched the ex-headmaster as he knocked then entered the cottage, the way a good friend would. The way a friend would. A friend and superior, who had taken advantage of a widow's vulnerability years earlier and made inappropriate romantic overtures to Bess. When she had refused him, he had turned to Jane Fellows, who had proven to be a more willing partner.

CHAPTER 14

Pete and Greta had the group assembled in the inn's green parlor to the left of the front door. The inn's staff had brought in extra chairs to accommodate everyone. All eyes turned to Demaris as he entered and nodded to his detectives. "All here?"

"All but Miss Johnson, sir," Greta said. "But she'll be back shortly. She's just stepped out to the…" Her eyes looked toward the hallway, the doors with *Ladies* and *Gentlemen* clearly visible.

"Excellent, thank you, Detective Burke."

As he spoke, the lady in question stepped back into the parlor and took a seat beside her partner, Christa Scott. He had taken a few minutes to read through the hastily scribbled notes Pete had given him earlier and knew that the two women were attorneys from Boston, partners in the firm as well as in life. He took a moment to gaze around the parlor, its faded Victorian décor, and uncomfortable chairs and sofas a strange backdrop for the group, most of whom were dressed casually in jeans or athletic clothes. Stewart, the jogger from Concord, New Hampshire, opened his mouth as if to speak, but then thought better of it.

Demaris stood framed in the doorway. He preferred to sit, but suspected this occasion was best tackled upright. "Thank you for coming. I know today has been very upsetting. I apologize for having to keep you here, but until we've had time to take everyone's statements and assess the situation, we have to ask you to remain, at least through the weekend."

"You mean it could be longer?" The voice came from the back of the room. He leaned against the window and the sunlight obscured his face.

"Mr.?"

"Littlefield, Carrion Littlefield. Just arrived today so I cannot imagine what I would have to contribute."

Demaris shielded his eyes, endeavoring to get a clear look at the slim, dark-haired man. "And your reason for coming to the Mystery Weekend?"

"I'm a publisher. Have been publishing Anne Greyson on the Littlefield Group's platform for a number of years. Couldn't pass up the opportunity to finally meet her, or him, as we've now come to learn."

"You published the books and you've never met the author?"

"Everything's electronic, no need. And, now, as I said, what possible relevance could I have to this investigation when I arrived at noon today?"

Irritated that he had been drawn into a conversation which should have occurred during a one-on-one interview, Demaris said, "Well, thank you, Mr. Littlefield, but we'll determine who and what's relevant. We'd be grateful for your patience."

A small hand crept up, attached to a diminutive brunette in her mid-thirties. She was dressed in beige wool skirt and matching sweater, a paisley scarf at her neck. The get-up reminded him of the way Bess Dore dressed, before the appearance of her dashing fiancé. He smiled and nodded at her. "Is it true?"

"Excuse me, Ms.?"

"Conlon, Wilma Conlon. I'm a librarian from Northport. Is it true that Mr. Winthrop was Anne Greyson?"

"Yes."

Her hand covered her mouth, and tears welled in her pale green eyes. He wanted to ask whether the obviously grief-stricken librarian knew Harry Winthrop, but instead gave her a sympathetic look and turned to the whole group. "We will be commencing the interviews immediately, so we ask that you stay in your respective establishments. One of the officers will find you when it's your turn."

Pete and Greta began circling the room, handing each guest a paper. "Detectives Dugan and Burke are distributing a list of the order in which we will interview all guests. The weekend organizers have informed us that dinner will go on as planned, albeit without the festivities and mystery focus. What I suggest is that you all go to dinner and we will locate you as needed. It is our intention to begin calling people during the cocktail hour, then leave you alone during the meal and return as you are finishing up your dessert. We have scheduled interviews until ten p.m. and will resume at nine a.m. tomorrow. If your allotted time is a hardship for you, I ask that you speak to one of my detectives and we will try to accommodate you. Any questions?"

A tall, slender woman stood from one of the folding chairs parked around the perimeter of the room. Dressed in flowing black yoga pants and soft green heather tunic, she appeared to be in her late fifties or early sixties. She was what one might call a handsome woman. "Yes, Detective, I have a question."

Ignoring the slight to his title, he said, "And, you would be?"

"Claire Rubin, from Mattapoisett. I'm here with my women's book club. I believe we've met at some point since you were with the local police for so many years. You grew up here, too, I believe? What I mean to say is, our group came together and we've been together all day, since early morning. There are eight of us in total and I cannot imagine there is anything we could contribute. As I'm sure is true with everyone here, we are eager to get home to our families and loved ones."

"Thank you, Ms. Rubin."

"Mrs."

"Mrs. Rubin, thank you. As I said, we'll be as expedient as we are able, but this is a homicide investigation and we want to be thorough and careful. What I can do is ask your group of eight to step into the other parlor for a moment, to speak with Detective Dugan. Could you do that, please? The rest of you are free to go to your rooms, dinner, or a short stroll around the village, as long as you let one of the officers know where you're going. Is that clear?"

With a smile, he nodded and turned away motioning to Pete and Greta. They followed him into the hall. "Greta, I'd like to see the guest house behind the Tavern, but first, Pete, when this book group comes out, find out their times and locations this morning. If they were, indeed, in a pack, or together, even a couple of them, it might be useful to talk to them together. Then, depending on what we hear, we can follow up with individuals, if necessary. Comprende?"

Dugan nodded. "Where will you be, boss?"

Demaris stared at the dispersing crowd. "I'm going to head over with Greta."

He nodded at Burke and they disappeared down the hall to the inn's back door.

CHAPTER 15

Demaris and Greta Burke sat at a long parsons table, which had been brought from the Tavern's barn and set up in the guest cottage that now served as their base of operations. Megan and her team had accompanied Harry Winthrop's body to the county clinic in Northport, where a lab had been made available to them. It was after five and Pete had not yet returned from the inn.

"Will you stay?"

His third in command looked up from a pile of papers and notes, her hazel eyes rimmed with dark circles, flaxen hair tied back in a haphazard ponytail, errant strands falling over the collar of her hooded gray sweatshirt. "No, sir, if it's all right, I'd like to go home, at least tonight. I'm trying to get coverage for my mom, but no one was available tonight."

Her seventy-year-old wheelchair-bound mother suffered from a host of ailments from emphysema to severe arthritis. Visiting nurses and home help aides took care of much of her daily care, but her daughter had moved in with her three years earlier and the night shift fell mostly to her. Greta was very private, but did confide in Pete. According to him, her brother, who lived in Florida, had recently begun to lend a modicum of support, but Pete described Gary Burke as "mostly a waste of space."

"Go home. Pete and I can handle tonight. Get a good night's sleep, sort out your mother's care, and come back tomorrow."

"I'm fine, sir, honest. I'll stay 'til ten, then head out. My brother's helping to line up caregivers for the next week. I should be able to stay starting tomorrow if needed."

Ice blue eyes studied her, kindness and concern evident in his gaze. "How long has it been since you slept?"

'Two, maybe three years. I'm used to it, sir." Tears rimmed her eyes and one snaked down her cheek.

In an uncharacteristic gesture, Demaris reached across and took her hand. "Go home, Greta. It's an order. I need you sharp tomorrow."

"But—"

"No buts. Pete and I'll take the interviews tonight. That local kid, Stevens, can assist. Can you be back by nine, do you think?"

She rose and grabbed her backpack. "Yes, sir, of course, sir. Thank you. These are my notes. I'll leave them here, but I've already gone over them with Pete. I can call when I—"

"Burke, we'll manage. Go." He smiled warmly, then grabbed reading glasses and began to sift through her notes. He wondered how Bess was faring.

Shortly after Greta's departure, Dugan came in, threw a duffle bag in the corner, and came to join him at the table.

"You staying here, then?"

"Someone should, don't you think? Did I just see Greta driving out of town?"

"I sent her home. She'll be back in the morning."

Dugan nodded and decided not to inquire further. Unlike Greta Burke, he looked ready to run a marathon. His dark gray slacks and light blue dress shirt had nary a wrinkle. He had tossed his gray wool sports jacket on top of the duffle and loosened his tie, but otherwise, he was immaculate. In his mid-thirties, his second-in-command looked like a teenager, his freckled face open and usually completely unguarded. Demaris had tried over the years to instill in his assistant the value of assuming a poker face. To date, his efforts had been unsuccessful. Dugan stared at his boss, blue eyes full of concern. "Are you staying?"

"Not tonight. We'll see how things go."

"They're starting to head over for cocktails at the Tavern."

"Good. Where's Stevens?"

"I sent him to the B&B to keep track of them. He says Chief Wilbur comes back tomorrow."

"Great, just what we need."

"You thinking of asking for help from the local guys?"

"Maybe, but I'd rather not if I can avoid it. I like young Stevens, but the farther Wilbur is from this investigation, the better. I think once Greta sorts her mother out, we can handle it, but I'll call in and see if I can get a floater or two in the morning. Give Stevens a call. I'd like to talk to him, feel him out, before I decide whether to keep him. He can help us tonight anyway, shuttling people back and forth."

Dugan reached for his cell and made the call. "He's on his way."

"Good, Greta's made a list of the locals. It's pretty long. We'll need to set up those interviews for tomorrow. There are a lot of school and townspeople on it. While I talk with Stevens, you can run over and get Ms. Reynolds. She's first on the list, correct?"

"I can stay till you're through with Stevens, then send him."

Demaris looked up from the notes and gave his assistant a sharp look. "If I'd wanted you to stay, I'd have suggested it."

"Yes, sir."

Stevens arrived shortly after Dugan's departure. He knocked, then opened the door tentatively and peered around.

Demaris waved him in. "Come in, Officer Stevens. Don't be shy. Want coffee or something?"

"No, thank you, sir."

"Sit, please."

"Thank you, sir." The young officer took a seat across from him.

"How long have you been in?"

"One month, sir."

"Old Harbor's your first job, then?"

"Yes, sir, graduated from the Academy in September."

"You live in town?"

"Northport, born and bred. My family runs the dairy farm."

"Ah, no wonder I haven't seen you before."

"Yes, sir. I know of you, sir. Everyone does."

"All bad, I'm guessing?"

Stevens blushed crimson. "Oh, no, sir, you're a legend in the village."

Demaris smiled. "I very much doubt that. Anyway, I asked to speak with you because we can use your help with this case, if you're willing?"

"Yes, sir, I mean, if Chief Wilbur agrees."

"With your permission, I'd like to talk with him and ask if we could borrow you for a few weeks. Didn't want to speak with him without asking you first."

"Of course, sir. I'd be honored."

Demaris smiled warmly, regarding the young officer for a moment. "The thing is, Brendan, it is Brendan, isn't it?"

"Yes, sir."

"If you join our group, we will ask for confidentiality. There can be no reports to Chief Wilbur or your fellow officers here in town. And, it goes without saying that you do not discuss the case with anyone without authorization from me. Is that clear?"

"Yes, sir."

"Do you think you can do that, son? After all, Chief Wilbur is your boss and he will be curious as will the townspeople and your peers. I will, of course speak with the Chief and explain this, but that doesn't mean he won't ask you what's going on. It's a lot of pressure for a junior officer."

Stevens sat ramrod straight in his seat. "Don't worry about me, sir. I am up to the task. I will not let you down."

Doesn't know Chief Wilbur well enough, Demaris mused, but nodded. He liked Stevens and trusted him. He would be a huge help. "Excellent. I will speak with the Chief tomorrow. The office knows you're helping tonight, do they not?"

"Yes, sir."

"No need for you to say anything until I talk with him, okay?"

"Yes, sir, thank you, sir."

"Very well. Take this dinner order for Detective Dugan and myself over to the Tavern and add something for yourself. You can wait until it's ready, then come straight back. We should be interviewing, but just come right in. Understood?"

"Yes, sir, thank you, sir."

Demaris extended his hand, which his companion shook firmly. "Welcome to the team, Officer Stevens. Now, off you go. I'm hungry."

Demaris smiled, watching the young man's retreat, then sat back and rubbed his eyes. It had been a long day and his allergies had kicked up. His doctor, who had a naturopath degree as well as an MD, had given him a concoction of therapeutic oils, which had changed his life, but the bottle sat on his dresser, twenty miles away. He made a note to retrieve it tonight whenever he managed to get home.

He thought about his many years serving as an Old Harbor police officer, then detective, then sergeant, the last eight under the command of Chief Ron Wilbur. Harry Winthrop Senior was absolutely right in his assessment of the man. He was "an incompetent buffoon." He had not put in an honest day's work in all the years he had known him and had only been promoted because his uncle ran the Town Council and no one dared cross him. Since the man was lazy, he allowed his officers free rein and rarely meddled in the day-to-day running of the station.

When Milt Wickie, the comptroller at Old Harbor Friends School had been murdered last year, Chief Wilbur had gladly turned over the case to Roger Demaris, who outranked him as a Detective Sergeant. He was no doubt ecstatic to know that R.H.D. had been called in so he wouldn't have to be bothered. That didn't mean that he would stay out of things, however. The indolent Chief loved gossip. Demaris did not look forward to the conversation with his former boss.

Absently, he pushed Greta's pile of notes and paperwork aside and pulled out his phone. Jane Fellows answered, her voice a whisper. "How is she?" he said.

"Sleeping. Says she's going to the dinner, but I'm not going to wake her. The phone's ringing might have done it."

"Sorry."

"How's the investigation going?"

"Just getting started. If you can spare a few minutes, I'd like to talk with you tonight. We're in the Tavern guest house. I'll be here until after ten. I don't want you to leave her alone. Only if you can get coverage."

"I'll try. I think I hear her stirring. If she does come to the dinner, I'll try to pop by."

"Thank you."

Jane hung up, sitting quietly by the phone, thinking. She was one of the few people who knew about Bess and Roger Demaris' past relationship. Bess and Roger had grown up in Northport, not Old Harbor, and had attended the regional high school twelve miles up the coast so their past was not widely known, if at all, in the village. I wonder, she thought, tapping the phone table.

CHAPTER 16

"I don't suppose I can get a refill when this is empty?" Liz Reynolds said, waving her martini glass at them.

Harry Winthrop's assistant stretched languidly on the room's love set, Pete beside her in one of the upholstered side chairs and Demaris directly in front of her in a straight-backed wooden chair. She had changed for dinner and now wore a shimmering, dark green sheath, six-inch silver heels and pendulous, sparkling silver earrings. Her blond hair was swept back, falling over her bare shoulders, and she had let her wrap, a silvery, diaphanous thing, fall to her waist.

"I assure you, Ms. Reynolds, this won't take long and you'll be back to the festivities in no time."

"Festivities? How can you say that when dear Harry is dead?" She dabbed at her dry eyes, flipping her hair back.

"Of course, you were close."

"Yes, very close. I've been his assistant for almost ten years."

"Still?"

She paused in her fidgeting to stare at the brooding, and she had to admit, handsome policeman. "Excuse me?"

"Sorry, I mean, are you still his assistant?"

"Absolutely."

'What exactly were your duties?"

"A little bit of everything. For one, he needs a presence in Boston, and I handle all the copyediting, cover design, whatever."

"Yourself?"

"Well, I supervise. I have a network of editors and designers. We do it all in-house first, then see what the publisher dreams up. If we don't like it, Harry's contract specifies that he has final approval of all layouts and cover designs."

"That's a bit unusual, isn't it?"

"When you have his kind of money, you can pretty much do anything. Without the Anne Greyson books and a few other mildly successful authors, Mount Hope Press, his current imprint, would be twiddling their fingers."

"Oh, is there anyone from Mount Hope here this weekend?"

"No, they only have like two employees. Strictly mom-and-pop operation, but Harry's been very loyal to them. I've been after him to go completely indie as I think he'd make more money, but he refuses, refused, to leave them. His books sell incredibly well through Carrion's group."

"You mean Mr. Littlefield?"

"Yes, his company is strictly e-books and he's making a fortune. Do you know they've been in business less than five years? Talk about being in the right place at the right time. The e-books industry has exploded, as you're no doubt aware."

Pete stared from his boss to Liz Reynolds, ready to explode. Demaris had yet to touch upon the case and seemed mired in trivial nonsense. He opened his mouth to ask a question, but then thought better of it and remained silent.

Demaris glanced over, reading his assistant's mood. He was following his gut, which was telling him that Harry Winthrop's death had nothing to do with the village or local issues, but he was groping the dark, uncertain where the light might creep in. "So is it fair to say that you are, or were, Mr. Winthrop's Girl Friday?"

"I find that term offensive, Lieutenant. I was his executive assistant."

"Excuse me. Aside from the logistics of bringing the books to print, did you assist Mr. Winthrop in other ways?"

"How do you think the books get publicized? I work with his publisher to make sure Anne Greyson is out there."

"So, is it safe to say that your duties in regards to Harry Winthrop were focused solely on his books?"

Again, she paused, this time, sitting up straighter and setting her empty glass on the cherry coffee table. "Just what are you implying?"

"I'm not implying anything. I'm simply asking whether you assisted Harry Winthrop in other ventures or in other aspects of his life."

"Well, I was his main point of contact in the U.S. while he was off gallivanting around the globe."

"Anything else?"

"I've planned the occasional gathering. Dinner parties, launch parties, whatever he needed."

"I see. How often was that?"

"Maybe once or twice a year."

"Did you act as hostess for these gatherings?"

"Sometimes, not always. I do have other clients, you know."

"Oh?"

"I consult for a few select people like Harry, helping with logistics of their businesses."

"All writers?"

"No."

"I'll need a list of those people, especially any who might have crossed over with your work with Mr. Winthrop."

As he spoke, Stevens stepped in with a box of food, which he set on the counter leading to the kitchen. Demaris nodded to him and he came to take a seat at the table just behind them.

"There aren't any cross-overs, except Carrion, who approached me recently. About part-time work."

"What kind of work?"

"I'm not sure because I hadn't given him an answer. He wondered if I might give him ten hours a week, and I said I'd think about it. I wanted to clear it with Harry and intended to talk with him about it this weekend. Oh, God, I can't believe he's gone."

Tears rimmed her steely blue eyes and she brushed them away, nodding thanks as Pete handed her a box of tissues.

Demaris waited several minutes for her to collect herself before speaking. "So, you've been to Old Harbor before?"

"Only twice. Harry and I mostly communicated by phone and e-mail. He came to Boston at least twice a month, sometimes more frequently."

"Did you have an intimate relationship with Mr. Winthrop?"

She set down the tissue box and stared at him. "No, it would have complicated our professional relationship."

"Small price to pay if—"

She waved her hand. "All right, all right, I wanted one, he didn't."

"Was this an issue?"

"No, we explored it, talked about it and decided it would be a mistake."

"And, when was this?"

"Shortly after Stella's death."

"The fiancée?"

"Do you know about Stella? She died in a car crash seven years ago."

He nodded.

"He was driving. The accident was not his fault."

"So I've been told," he said quietly, recalling details of the accident, which had come to light during an earlier case involving another murder.

"Poor Harry was devastated. I tried to comfort him and one thing led to another. We slept together once, if that's what you're after, but it was a long time ago, several months after the accident."

"Prior to this weekend, had you met Mr. Winthrop's current fiancée?"

"Yes, once, very briefly, when I was at the hall dropping something off. Mousy little thing, if you ask me. Haven't a clue what he saw in her."

"Had he asked you to handle any of the arrangements for the wedding?"

"No, and to be honest, I was offended after all I've done for him. Never thought it would happen anyway."

"Oh, and why is that?"

"She wasn't his type."

"And what type was that?"

"Glamorous, accomplished, a high profile woman, socially prominent, professionally successful. Not some middle-aged schoolmarm from east Podunk."

"Were you jealous of Bess Dore, Ms. Reynolds?" It was the first time he had used Bess' name and he wondered if she would pretend not to know of whom he spoke.

"Are you insane? That dowdy little nobody? Hardly."

"From what I understand, he was deeply in love with her."

Anger flashed in eyes that now seemed black as coal. "Is this really what you want to ask me about? Whether I killed Harry so no one else could have him?"

"Where were you early this morning?"

"Driving down from Boston. I attended that god-awful reception last night because he asked me to, but went home to gather some things. As you may recall, I arrived back shortly after noon, and poor Harry had been dead several hours by then."

"And, you would know this because?"

"Because it's been all over the fucking village, for God's sake!"

"Can anyone verify when you left Boston?"

"I live alone and the doorman for my building was on break when I left, so, no, I guess not. But the idea that I would harm dear Harry is preposterous. I loved him and would never harm a hair on his head. Yes, I didn't approve of Ms. Dore, but I was happy for him. Much as I hate to admit it, he's been happier since he met her than he's been in all the years I've known him."

"Can you think of someone who might want to harm him? Someone with whom he had quarreled, perhaps?"

"No, everyone loved him. Did you know him?"

"Yes."

"Then you understand. He was a warm, kind, and generous man." Demaris nodded. "And, I intend to stay right here in this Godforsaken outpost until you find out who killed him."

"That may be a while."

"I've booked a room at the inn indefinitely."

"I see. Do you know if anyone acquainted with Mr. Winthrop was an archer?"

"No, and if you're asking, I tried it once and couldn't hit the broad side of a barn."

"Well, thank you, Ms. Reynolds. You've been very helpful. Officer Stevens will escort you over to dinner. If you think of anything, please be in touch with one of us. Detective Burke will return in the morning so you can feel free to speak with her, Detective Dugan, Officer Stevens, or myself. Beyond that, I would ask that you not discuss the case with anyone."

She rose, and ran fingers through her hair before smoothing her dress, which was now creased and wrinkled. "I'll be keeping close tabs on things. If you're not making progress finding Harry's killer, I will not hesitate to hire professional help."

"One minute, if you please? Were you aware that Mr. Winthrop fancied himself an amateur sleuth?"

Hand on hip, towering above them now, she gazed down, expression haughty. "He was far from an amateur, my dear lieutenant. He helped a number of people out of very sticky situations. And, I understand he saved your ass last year with the death at the school."

Dugan started to speak, to defend his boss, but a look from Demaris silenced him.

"We'll need a list of any person with whom he consulted or assisted in this capacity and if you have any information about the nature of their problems, I hope you will be forthcoming. Perhaps you would be so good as to create such a description along with the list of your other clients. One of the officers will stop by the inn in the morning to collect it."

"Of course, I'll get right on it," she said, her voice dripping with sarcasm as she stooped to retrieve her empty glass, her breasts nearly falling out of her dress. "Ta ta, gentlemen."

"So much for grieving," Pete muttered as the door closed behind the pair.

"Go after them, will you? I want to talk to Littlefield next, then Stewart and his lady friend. Ask Stevens to come back quickly so he can eat, then you and I can eat after we talk to Littlefield."

As Dugan grabbed his jacket, the door opened and Bess walked in. Demaris stood up and came to greet her. "Bess, what are you doing out? Jane said you were sleeping."

Before she could answer, Pete said, "I can stay, sir."

"No, you can't. Off with you. You need to catch up to Stevens, now."

His warning look stifled any further discussion and Dugan departed, with one backward gaze at his boss, whose eyes were on her.

CHAPTER 17

"Here, sit down. Can I get you something?"

"No, thanks," she said, taking a seat on the loveseat recently vacated by Liz Reynolds. "Have you learned anything?"

"Bess, you should be at home, not here."

Her hand shot up. "Don't, Roger! Please don't treat me like I'm some feeble-minded imbecile."

He grabbed hold of the straight-backed chair, and pulled it to sit in front of her, shoving the coffee table to the side. "I'm not patronizing you, I'm trying to support you. Your fiancé was murdered today. You should be grieving, not wandering around the village."

"I'm not wandering around the village. I've come to see you, then I'll be making a brief appearance at the dinner."

"The dinner, why?"

"Because someone connected to this weekend event should be there."

Risking rebuke, he reached forward and took her hands. "They're just eating, Bess. There's no longer an event."

Her hands were cold and she trembled, but did not pull away. When he looked up, he saw tears snaking down her pale cheeks.

"Bess, let me take you home, please? Or, I can call Jane."

She shook her head violently from side to side. "No, no, I can't go home! I can never go home. Oh, Roger, who would want to hurt him?"

He moved beside her on the sofa and put his arm around her shoulders. She's lost weight, he mused as Bess crumpled against him, sobbing. This was how Dugan and Stevens found them fifteen minutes later when they returned without Carrion Littlefield, their next interviewee. Shock and concern registered on Pete's face, but he wisely kept quiet, waiting for his boss to speak. "Where's Littlefield?"

"Didn't come for cocktail hour. Stayed in his room to take a call. He told them he'd be at dinner by six and it's quarter after now."

"Okay, let's eat. It's gonna be a long night." He waved them toward the kitchen and turned back to her. "Bess, we got sandwiches from the Tavern. There are plenty. Have something to eat, or drink, at least, will you?"

She shook her head.

"If you don't eat and drink something, I'm driving you home and getting someone to keep you there. If you'll try to have something, I'll walk you over to the dinner myself."

Reluctantly, she rose and joined them at the counter. Perched on a stool beside Stevens, she nibbled at a chicken salad sandwich and ate a few chips. "Want a soda or something, Ms. Dore?" Stevens asked.

"Thanks, Brendan. I'd love one of those bottles of water."

He hopped off his stool and grabbed a water, then sat beside her again.

"So, they've pulled you into this, have they?"

"Yes, Miss. I'm so sorry for your loss. Mr. Winthrop was a great guy."

"Yes, he was."

Demaris watched them, fearful she would break down again, but the young officer's presence seemed to be comforting. As they talked, he pulled Pete aside and asked him to locate Jane Fellows as soon as he was finished with dinner. 'Then, find Littlefield and bring him here. You and Stevens can start the preliminary interview. Have him take notes."

"I could take her home."

"Is that what I asked you to do?"

"No, sir."

"Then finish your supper and get moving, okay?"

CHAPTER 18

By the time Roger and Bess reached the inn, everyone was seated and enjoying their pumpkin soup, artful swirls of crème fraiche in the shape of autumn leaves adorning the surface of each bowl's contents. Claire Rubin, self-appointed leader of the women's book group, waved to them. "Here, Bess, dear. We have an extra seat. Please come and sit with us."

Claire's children had attended Old Harbor Friends. She and her husband, Dicky had been loyal supporters of the school. She attended occasional athletic events and campus functions. Bess worked with Claire every year on the annual craft fair, a huge fundraiser for the school.

Bess smiled wanly and headed for the table, her companion at her side. "Just for a minute, Claire. I'm not staying. Just wanted to check in and say hello. Let me check with the staff and I'll come have soup, at least."

"Excellent. I'll ask them for a fresh bowl. What do you say, Detective? Shall we find a chair for you, too?"

"It's Lieutenant, Ms. Rubin, and thank you, but I've already eaten."

"You remembered my name. How flattering."

He nodded. "Ladies," and followed Bess to where Cathy and Lois stood at the pantry doorway. At Harry's insistence, the B & B owners had joined forces with the Inn's cook for the dinner.

"Bess, what in the world are you doing here?"

"I wanted to check in, to see if everything was going okay."

"Sweetheart," Lois said, reaching out to pat her arm. "Harry's gone. We're just keeping the captives fed until Roger releases them. There's no reason for you to play host."

Bess leaned against him and both women stared from one to the other. "I'll sit with Claire and the book group, have a bowl of soup, then head home."

"Yes," Cathy said, drolly. "Commander Rubin has ordered the wait staff to bring a fresh bowl."

"Thank you both for handling this."

"Have you got someone to stay with you, sweetheart? Cathy or I could come out after the crowd disperses?"

"Thank you, but Jane's just gone home to collect some things. She'll stay with me until my mother arrives tomorrow."

That explained how Bess had been able to escape from her usually vigilant friend, Demaris thought, eyes scanning the crowd. Jane had probably left her sleeping and the minute she had driven away, Bess had hopped up and rushed out.

"Are you joining us for soup, Lieutenant?" Cathy asked.

"Thanks, but no. I've got to get back to the guest house." When he turned, Bess had left his side and was headed to the book group's table. As she progressed, she paused briefly at each table to say hello.

Lois studied their old friend, his eyes betraying the intensity of his feelings. Poor Roger, she thought, still madly in love with Bess Guilford after all these years. "She won't give up, will she?"

He smiled and shook his head. "If she gives up, she'll collapse. I suspect she fears the grieving may destroy her."

"Hope it doesn't last another ten years," Cathy said, turning away to help at the sideboard.

"She's tough, Roger. She'll survive. Let's get her through the funeral, then she can collapse surrounded by friends. When does Mommy Dearest arrive?"

"Sometime tomorrow, I believe."

"Not sure if that's good or bad, but Maggie's a good sport and will be invaluable in planning the service."

Demaris had only vague recollections of Maggie Guilford and they were not pleasant ones. Maggie had never approved of him when he and Bess were dating. After he broke her daughter's heart, she had never spoken another word to him. He felt a tug on his sleeve and turned to find the librarian from Northport standing behind him.

"Detective, could I have a word?"

"Good evening, Ms. Conlon. I believe we are scheduled to interview you in the morning."

"I know, but I have to speak to you tonight, now, please."

With a glance toward the book group and Bess, he said, "Very well, but it will have to be quick as I'm needed elsewhere."

He led her out of the dining room to one of the inn's parlors, now deserted. After they had seated themselves side by side on a very uncomfortable Victorian settee, he said, "Now, then, how can I help?"

"I really have nothing to add to your investigation. I was very fond of Harry Winthrop and couldn't shoot a bow and arrow if I tried. Might I be permitted to leave in the morning? My cats need me. There's no one to watch them. I am not far away. You and your detectives can find me anytime."

"Is someone caring for them tonight?"

"Excuse me?"

"Your cats."

"Oh, yes, my neighbor, but I don't want to impose. If I might just have my interview tonight and head home I would be most grateful."

"I understand your dilemma, Ms. Conlon, but we cannot conduct your interview until morning, I'm sorry. There is an order to things and we will follow it. I understand that Mr. Winthrop was a frequent visitor at your library?"

"Yes, two or three times a week. He was researching for a book."

"Perhaps tonight you might make some notes about the nature of his research and the approximate frequency and duration of his visits. I should think that after your interview, you might be able to head home because, as you say, we can locate you easily, but let's wait until morning to determine this, okay?"

"But, I—"

"Now, I really must get back to my officers, and you, to the main course, I should think?"

Her face registered displeasure, but she accepted his hand and rose to accompany him back to the dining room where they parted company. He spied Jane at the far corner of the room talking with Lois at the sideboard and waved. After a quick glance at Bess and the book club, he crossed the room and nodded to Jane.

"She gave me the slip."

"It appears so. Will you stay with her tonight?"

"Absolutely. She will not get out of my sight again until her mother's arrival, I promise."

"Who's collecting Mrs. Guilford from the airport?"

"I believe a friend of hers from Mattapoisett."

"I'll be off, then. Take care of her."

Jane smiled at him. "Don't worry. Good luck."

CHAPTER 19

When he returned to the guest house, Pete was in the midst of a conversation with the publisher, Carrion Littlefield, Stevens seated nearby taking notes. Littlefield had taken one of the side chairs and Pete the loveseat. Right away, this gave the interviewee a height advantage. They all looked up as Demaris entered and hung his coat on one of the brass hooks by the door.

"Well, it's about time, Superintendent. It's been fun sitting here with the second string, but can we get this over with so I can have dinner?"

"It's Lieutenant, Mr. Littlefield. We're sorry to disrupt your dinner, but under the circumstances, we have no choice. This is a murder investigation and I suspect that no one, including you, will starve."

He had meant to keep his tone neutral, but could see by Stevens' wide-eyed expression that he had not succeeded. Littlefield on the other hand was completely unfazed and sat languidly in his chair as if he were posing for a spread in *GQ*.

Dugan stood. "Just started, boss. We have established that Mr. Littlefield arrived in the village around noon and heard about Mr. Winthrop's death shortly after he checked in at the inn. He has been publishing the Anne Greyson books for five years."

"Thanks, Pete. Sit back down and continue. I'm fine here." He pulled up a straight-backed chair and sat to Littlefield's left, Pete to the right and Stevens behind them.

Dugan sat down and consulted his notebook. "You were saying about how you and Mr. Winthrop met?"

"As I told you, we have never met. I'm a publisher. She or he writes books. They may be drivel, but they're popular drivel."

"You mean to say that you never met Anne Greyson or Mr. Winthrop?"

"That would be correct. It's all electronic, as I told you earlier. Only person with whom I ever communicated was that assistant of his, the Reynolds woman."

"And, you publish books, even if you don't like them?"

"My dear Officer Dugan, I'm an e-books publisher. Do you know how cutthroat that business is? If I only published books I like, I'd be on the streets peddling hot dogs."

Demaris cleared his throat. "It's Detective Dugan, Mr. Littlefield. We'll get back to your publishing activities in a minute, if you don't mind. Can anyone verify your whereabouts this morning?"

"As a matter of fact, no. I left the city around ten thirty and drove straight here."

"No Boston traffic?"

"No."

"Which way do you come?"

"I haven't a clue what relevance this could possibly have, but I came down ninety-five through Providence. I had thought to stop at a coffee shop I like on the East Side of Providence, but then was running late so I kept going."

Demaris glanced at Stevens, who made a note to check traffic reports from the morning. "So you could have arrived at six a.m. for all we know."

"I can't imagine why in the world I would do such a thing, but yes, I suppose you're right."

"Are you a jogger?"

"Yes."

"Archer?"

"If you mean, have I ever tried to shoot a bow and arrow, yes, when I was at Boy Scout camp decades ago. I was very bad at it, if you must know. And, why in the world would I want to harm one of my best-selling authors?"

"Maybe the drivel became unbearable?"

"Is that some kind of a joke?"

"Do you know anyone who might have wanted to harm Mr. Winthrop?"

"You mean, do I know anyone who might have wanted to harm the mediocre spinster writer, Anne Greyson? Absolutely not. Maybe someone discovered the deception and was pissed?"

"Like you?" Dugan asked.

Before Littlefield could respond, Demaris said, "That'll be all for now, Mr. Littlefield. Officer Stevens will accompany you back to the inn."

He sat up, surprised at the abrupt conclusion of their conversation. "Thank you, but I don't need a babysitter, Lieutenant."

"No trouble, sir," Stevens said, as he stood and grabbed his jacket.

"Coming to get the next victim, I expect?"

"Have a nice dinner." Demaris smiled, turning his back, Littlefield clearly dismissed.

"So, I'm free to head home tomorrow?"

"I'm afraid not. Let's see how the day goes. We'll keep you posted. For now, I'd reserve your room for a day or two anyway."

Stevens held the door and Littlefield stormed out.

"My money's on him, boss. What a prick."

"Yes, but a prick without a motive. What do we know about the book seller? He's next, I believe."

Pete pulled out Greta's notes on Boyle Wolfson, the owner of a bookshop in Cambridge that specialized in mysteries and began reading them aloud. Fifteen minutes later, Stevens returned, alone.

"Where the hell is Wolfson?" Pete asked.

"Gone. Left after his soup and didn't come back."

Pete stood, slapping the counter. "Jesus Christ, Stevens, did you check his room?"

"Yes, sir, he's staying at the B&B, but no sign of him there. Owners are at the inn, of course, but they had keys and I checked. All his stuff's still there, but he isn't."

Demaris set aside the notes and peered over his glasses first at the young officer, then at Dugan. "Okay, you two. Off you go. Check around the village. Maybe he went for a walk or into one of the shops."

"Not many open now, sir, except the Apothecary and gas station."

"What about his car?"

"The B&B doesn't take people's registration and they didn't notice what he drove."

"Pete, that should be in Greta's notes. Check first, then you two go."

"What about you?" Pete said, already shuffling papers.

"I'm going to check the Tavern. See if he went for a drink. If I find him, I'll text you."

"Dark green Saab," his assistant said, grabbing his jacket. "Come on, Stevens. Let's find the errant Mr. Wolfson."

CHAPTER 20

As Demaris grabbed his coat, he wondered if Pete Dugan had always been hotheaded and short-tempered, or if he had learned the counterproductive behavior from his mentor. As he stepped into the chill of the evening, he made a mental note to talk to his assistant. After so many years together, there was not much they could not say to each other.

The Tavern was full of villagers, many familiar to him. Its warmth beckoned and fires blazed in the enormous fireplaces in both rooms. He nodded at Peter and Carrie Thurbert as he headed for the bar. They were having dinner with another couple, both of whom were strangers.

The retired headmaster waved and beckoned to him. "Hello, Lieutenant!"

He glanced toward at the bar, where he spotted another stranger in worn tweed jacket and rumpled khakis. The missing Mr. Wolfson. He turned back to Thurbert to say hello.

"Hello, again," Thurbert. "You remember my wife, Carrie?"

"Yes, hello, nice to see you again, Ms. Thurbert."

She nodded, not looking particularly pleased to see him.

"And let me introduce you to Arthur Burnham and his friend Lana Wilkins. Art is Acting Head at the moment, while my successor, Pru Marsden, is away on a family emergency. Doing a crack up job of it, too."

Burnham rose and shook his hand. "Lieutenant, nice to meet you. I've heard so much about you."

"All bad, I fear," Demaris said, taking the outstretched hand. "Ms. Wilkins, nice to meet you, too."

"Well, well, now that I know this Godforsaken village has such gorgeous police officers, I'll plan to visit more often."

Her companion's sharp look was lost on the raven-haired siren. As she batted her eyelashes, Wilkins played with a silky scarf draped languidly around her slender neck. Swirls of blues and greens accented her green eyes and coordinated perfectly with her body-hugging cashmere sweater in soft mossy green. Full-figured is how one might describe Lana Wilkins, a sharp contrast to anorexic Carrie Thurbert, whose beige cable knit sweater hung on her like a burlap sack.

Thurbert laughed, a curt, quick snort that did not quite reach his eyes. "Lieutenant Demaris does not work in the village, Lana. He's head of R.H.D., one of the state's three elite homicide teams."

Although Demaris suspected that the lovely Lana and her companion were roughly the same age, he looked about ten years older, his sandy hair thinning slightly, tinged with gray. Lana's color, expertly applied, had no doubt come from a bottle. Athletic and trim, like Thurbert, the interim headmaster was dressed casually in corduroy slacks and a gray wool sweater, handsome in a Mr. Chips kind of way.

"Not sure about the elite part, but good to meet you both. I don't want to disturb your dinner."

"Nonsense," Thurbert said. "Sit and have a drink with us."

"Thank you, but I'm not free at the moment. I would like to talk with you, Mr. Burnham, when convenient. Would you be free either tomorrow or Monday?"

"I think Monday would be best, if that's okay? Just call my administrative assistant, Becky Sitwell. She keeps my schedule." He handed Demaris a card. "My office and cell numbers are there. I'm in residence at the Head's House until Pru Marsden returns. We could meet there in the evening, or during the day, if Becky puts you on my schedule."

"Thank you, goodnight, folks."

In the short time he had been in conversation, Wolfson had drunk what looked like four shots of whiskey, followed each time with a beer chaser. Thus, the man was face down on the dark mahogany bar, eyes closed. Cursing himself for lingering, he tapped his shoulder. "Mr. Wolfson?"

"Huh?" Gray bleary eyes looked up, unseeing.

"Okay, Mr. Wolfson, let's get you back to your room, shall we?" He laid hold of his right arm and dragged him to stand. Fortunately, he was thin and wiry. Demaris motioned to the bartender, a young kid in his twenties who looked vaguely familiar. He came around the bar, took Wolfson's left arm and together they dragged him toward the door.

"Here, Charlie, I'll take over. You go back to the bar."

Charlie Boardman, Demaris thought, grateful to Peter Thurbert as Wolfson was transferred to him. Charlie was Ralph's grown son, his father's pride and joy. Hadn't he heard the boy had gone to Brown? What the hell was he doing tending bar in Old Harbor?

Slowly, the three men wended their way across the street to the B&B. Halfway across, Thurbert wondered if Wolfson had left a heavier coat at the bar since he wore only his threadbare tweed jacket. "We'll get it later," Demaris muttered, taking slow, deep breaths to keep his temper in check. Fortunately, Lois had returned and opened Wolfson's room. After removing his jacket, they plunked him on the bed, removed his shoes, and closed the door behind him. Then, they bid Lois goodnight and headed back across the street.

"Guess there'll be no talking to him tonight," Thurbert said.

"Caught up with him too late. I was surprised to see Charlie Boardman back in town. Didn't he go to Brown?"

"Started there, but came home when his mother got sick. Very sad, such promise. After she died, he enrolled in UMass Dartmouth and is completing his engineering degree while working at the Tavern. Sometimes works events at the school, too."

"Nice kid."

"Yes, he is. Keeps Ralph going. He's never been the same since Nancy died, poor man."

"They both live on the Winthrop estate, then?"

"Yes, but as I understand it, Charlie often stays somewhere in town with buddies."

As they entered the warmth of the taproom, Charlie held up a tattered wool overcoat and scarf. "Thanks, Charlie. You, too, Thurbert." He grabbed the coat and headed out the side door that led to the guest house.

When he found the guest house empty, he checked his cell phone to find it had been on vibrate and he had failed to feel it through his thick wool jacket. "Dammit," he muttered, finding six missed calls from Pete. He dialed his assistant, who answered immediately.

"Where the hell are you?"

"We're at Winthrop Hall, sir."

"Who's we? You and Stevens?"

"Yes, sir."

"Are you going to tell me why before moss grows over my shoes?"

"It's Ralph Boardman, boss."

"What's happened?"

"He's dead."

"How?"

"Pitch fork through his back."

"I'll be right there."

"Yes, sir."

CHAPTER 21

"Poor bastard never knew what hit him." Dugan stood back, giving space to his superior.

As he bent down, Demaris spied Stevens crouched green-faced in the corner. Dugan mimicked vomiting.

"Where's Megan?"

"She's on her way. Should be here soon."

"Jesus Christ, what a mess. Poor man, we should have protected him."

"You think it's the same killer?"

Demaris nodded How were Boardman and Winthrop connected? Had Ralph seen the killer? He had made a huge tactical mistake and was struggling to maintain composure lest he end up crouching in the corner alongside Stevens.

The barn lighting consisted of a few overhead fixtures. The local police had set up additional crime scene lights, which were placed at odd angles, bathing the space in uneven, fractured light. Boardman lay face down, an ancient pitchfork with splintery wooden handle pinning him to the earthen floor. Same flannel shirt, jeans, and duct-taped boots. The cry of a screech owl pierced the silence. Four local officers kept guard outside the door. The steam from their breathing created a small fog bank in the doorway, but no one dared speak.

An antique livestock barn, Mr. Winthrop had had it dismantled and moved to the property. The stalls served as repositories for tools, mowers, and other farm equipment. Boardman's apartment was above where they stood. A shaft of light shone from the stairway leading up to it.

"Who found him?"

"The cook, Mrs. Pierce. Apparently she brings him coffee at night after the old man goes to bed. They usually sit and chat awhile."

"Does the rest of the household know?"

She woke Mr. Winthrop. It's the housekeeper's night off. She's staying at her sister's in Northport."

"What about his son?"

"Not yet. I told the local guys to hold off until you got here."

"I'll go. Take Stevens upstairs and look around. As soon as I talk with Charlie, I'll be back. Tell Mr. Winthrop we'll speak in the morning."

"But—"

"But nothing. He certainly didn't put a pitchfork in Boardman's back and he was asleep, so he has nothing to contribute. Poor man lost his son this morning. Jesus Christ."

He motioned to one of the locals and asked for a ride. He could have easily driven himself, but he was headed for the worst part of the job. Notifications took so much out of a person. They had never gotten easier with the years. Regretting his supper, he followed a young female officer to her car.

Charlie Boardman was still behind the bar when they arrived. Rachel, the dining room manager, was not in sight so Demaris went into the kitchen where he found Tilly cleaning an enormous soup tureen. She appeared to be alone and he wondered where the rest of the staff were hiding.

"Well, this is a surprise, Lieutenant. Can we help you?"

"I need for you or someone, if anyone else is around, to take over for Charlie. I need to speak with him, after which he will be in no state to continue working."

"What's happened?" she asked, just as the back door opened and two kitchen workers appeared with empty trash bins, a wafting of nicotine in their wake.

"His father's dead. Can you please relieve him?"

"Of course." She threw her soiled apron on a stool, smoothed her unruly hair, and led the way back to the taproom.

Demaris had asked his driver to wait in the car. After relating the horrible news to Charlie Boardman, they drove him to the house where his aunt was visiting, a small cottage on the edge of the village. Charlie took the news with quiet stoicism, only breaking down when he spied his aunt, waiting with open arms.

"You know Charlie?" he asked as they drove back toward the Winthrop estate.

"We went to high school together," Vivian Pacheco said quietly. "He was much smarter than most of us." She stared straight ahead, her sharp, delicate features silhouetted in the moonlight. Tears glistened in her dark eyes, and she let them stay, tucking an errant stray of dark hair back under her cap as she parked the patrol car beside the barn.

"Thank you, Vivian," he said quietly as he stepped from the car. She nodded. "Yes, sir," but remained in her vehicle, uncertain of what to do next.

Megan Krieger and her assistant, Bethany Yuan, were there, crouched over the body. Face grim, Megan nodded to him.

"Time of death?"

"Probably an hour ago, maybe two. Died instantly. Fork pierced the heart and lungs."

"What's this wet spot?"

"Coffee. She dropped the tray when she found him."

"Anything else?"

"Not yet. Hard to find footprints on this floor. We'll check for prints on the handle."

"Where are the others?"

"Stevens is upstairs and Pete's in with Molly Pierce."

"Poor woman."

He turned away and headed for the house. The officers had roped off most of the yard leading up to the barn. They would check more carefully in the daylight. Demaris wasn't hopeful. He found Pete and Molly seated at the long, pine table, a tray with broken cups and sodden biscuits beside them.

Her eyes were puffy and her blue calico apron was stained with spilled coffee. She held what appeared to be a dishcloth in her hands which she was alternately wringing and dabbing at her chest.

"I'm so sorry for your loss, Molly." He sat beside her, his large hand covering her own. "Where is Mr. Winthrop?"

"In bed. The doctor's with him."

"Good."

"Has Detective Dugan taken down your statement?" She looked blank, but Pete nodded. "Good, let's get you to bed, then. I've had the officers call Helen home from her sister's. She should be here soon to stay with you."

"Where's poor Charlie?" she asked, breaking into sobs. "First his dear mother, now this."

"We've dropped him with his aunt, who happened to be house sitting for an old friend in the village." As he spoke the door to the hallway opened and Helen Stevens appeared, shrugging off her heavy coat and coming to embrace her coworker.

Demaris stood and greeted the housekeeper. "Ms. Stevens, thank you for coming. I think brandy may be in order and I'm certain Mr. Winthrop's doctor could prescribe something to help you both sleep."

"Of course, I'll take care of it."

"We'll leave you now. An officer is posted outside. Please call if you need us. We'll be back in the morning, okay?"

Demaris placed his card on the table and he and Pete headed back to the barn where they were removing Ralph Boardman on a stretcher, the pitchfork still embedded in his back.

CHAPTER 22

After two hours of sleep, the team assembled in the guest house at eight a.m. Demaris and Pete had shared the one bedroom, and he had sent Stevens home. Greta arrived with a bag and had headed to the B&B to see about the rooms for herself and her boss. Pete planned to remain at the guest house or commute from his apartment in Northport. The only one of them that looked vaguely rested was Greta.

"I want all the weekend people assembled at the inn at eleven. Get locals if you have to and round up every damn one of 'em."

His superior had lapsed into crude vernacular. Never a good sign. "What are you thinking, boss?"

"I'm thinking we need to narrow our lens. While I speak with them as a group, you two take Stevens and search every room."

"Get the forms, have them there for them to sign at eleven. If anyone resists, we'll keep them and get warrants."

"But, that might take hours."

"I've already phoned Judge Williams in Northport. After hearing about Boardman, he's faxing the warrants this morning, but I won't produce them except for the recalcitrant."

It was one of his boss' favorite stratagems, yet often not possible. Two murders in the tiny village in one day had changed the landscape a bit. Pete regarded his superior, his blue oxford shirt rumpled and stained, tie long abandoned. Dark circles rimmed his icy blue eyes, but his gaze was sharp and clear. Demaris needed a shave. "Want me to send someone to your place, get a few of your things, boss?"

Demaris gazed at him as if he had sprouted horns. The idea of anyone poking around his apartment was unthinkable and Pete knew it. "Thanks, Mother Hen, but I'm headed there after this. Will stop on my way back to check in with Megan."

CHAPTER 23

After packing a bag, Demaris headed back toward Old Harbor, detouring to the clinic in Northport, where he found Megan and Bethany taking a coffee break at a small table across the lab from the two bodies lying side by side on gurneys. Two more sleep-deprived souls. Dressed in white lab coats, they appeared to have been at it all night.

"Didn't either of you go home?"

"Soon, sir. We've finished up most of it. There's not much, I'm 'fraid."

"Time of death?"

"Sometime between seven and nine."

"You can't narrow it down?"

"The ground was cold. It's difficult."

"What else?"

"Well, I'd guess the killer was close to Boardman's height and relatively strong. The thrust was straight on, not upward or downward. No prints. Probably wore gloves."

"Did the sweep up yield anything?"

"Not so far, but the guys are there this morning," she said, pushing an errant hair back behind her ear. Both women had long, dark hair pulled back in ponytails that looked as if a two-year-old had tied them.

"Anything more on Winthrop?"

"The arrow was a beauty. Not from your run-of-the-mill archery set. Custom-made, by the look of it. We're doing a search for the manufacturer. Pierced his heart. Guy was either a great shot, or incredibly lucky. Mr. Winthrop never knew what hit him. He died instantly."

"That's something, at least. May bring comfort to his widow."

"I didn't know he was married."

Demaris shook himself. "Sorry, fiancée. Did they find anything around the spot where the killer hid?"

"It had been swept with a branch, to obscure footprints, but we did lift one corner of a print from a running shoe. I fear there'll be no way to tell what kind of shoe, but we've sent it out, just in case."

"Okay, thanks, ladies. Go home, get some sleep. If you hear anything, give Pete or me a call. Let's pray no more bodies turn up."

"Yes, sir," Krieger said, regarding her boss as he gazed with sad eyes at the lifeless forms in front of them.

CHAPTER 24

"How lovely of dear Peter to make the memorial arrangements so quickly, sweetie."

Maggie Guilford hovered over her daughter, as she picked at her toast and sipped tepid tea from a cracked cup. Her mother had been there for less than an hour, her suitcases still parked in the front hall, and she was already suffocating her. "Tomorrow at two, you say? Is there a dress shop where we can find you something suitable? I suppose it will have to be that dreadful mall in Northport."

Bess slumped on the living room couch, thinking how cold the room was. She rarely used the living room. Adjacent to the front hallway, it faced the driveway and was not nearly as cozy as the study with its French doors overlooking the fields and woods behind the cottage. "I have dresses, Mother."

"Absolutely not. I've already surveyed your closets. Besides, it will distract us from our grief. Where did you get those pajamas and bathrobe? They remind me of ones you had in college."

"They are."

"Oh, good Lord, I will add pajamas to the shopping list."

"Mother, please, I don't want to go shopping. I don't need to be distracted. Harry died yesterday, not last year."

"I know, sweetheart," she said, coming to cradle her daughter's shoulders in her arms. "Why are you holding your head like that? Are you ill?"

"Hungover."

"What?"

"The doctor gave me some kind of horse pills which Jane and Roger insisted I wash down with brandy."

Her mother sat back, gazing at her. "For sleep, I'd expect. So Roger Demaris has been here?"

"His team is investigating this."

"But why come here? Surely he doesn't think you had anything to do with it?"

"Mother, I can't do this right now." Bess rose to gaze out the window facing the drive. "Oh, my, speak of the devil. Your nemesis has just driven up."

Maggie Guilford peered over her daughter's shoulders and spied Demaris and his assistant stepping out of the jeep. "He's not my nemesis. I just don't trust the man."

"He's a police officer, for goodness' sake. Who could be more trustworthy?"

"That's not what I mean and you know it. Anyone who breaks my baby's heart does not endear himself to me."

What about you, breaking your daughter's heart with your disdain for Roger, rejection of Dad and me, and a host of other indignities? Bess thought, slipping out of her grasp. "Can you please answer the door? I want to change."

And so it was that the men were greeted by Maggie Guilford's smiling face instead of her daughter's. If Demaris was disappointed, his face did not betray it.

"Mrs. Guilford, how nice to see you again. This is my assistant, Detective Dugan."

Pete watched his boss, dumbfounded by his tone and the shy smile he gave the woman, who looked to be in her mid-sixties.

"You've come up in the world since I've seen you. What's it been, twenty-five years? I understand you are some kind of Inspector now?"

"Lieutenant, actually, we don't have inspectors and constables on this side of the Atlantic. I'm part of a regional homicide group."

"The Head of," Pete said, sensing a need to protect his boss from the force of nature standing in front of them.

She waved her hand. "Whatever you say, gentlemen. The point is, you escaped Old Harbor. That's a step in the right direction. Did I hear you are divorced?"

"Is Bess at home, Mrs. Guilford? We only have a few minutes."

"I'm here, Roger! Be just a sec," she called from the back of the house. And then she was in the hallway, stocking feet, soft brown shoes in hand, wearing jeans and a gray sweater. "Would you like coffee?"

"No, thanks, we only have a few minutes. Is there somewhere we can chat?"

Maggie Guilford waved toward the living room, but her daughter ignored her. "Of course, come back to the kitchen. Sorry it's such a mess."

They sat at the table, the men on one side, women on the other. "Mother, don't feel you have to stay if you'd like to unpack."

Refusing to take the hint, she patted Bess' arm. "I'm here for you, darling. The bags can wait."

So, Pete thought, each of them had their protector.

"Jane gone home?"

"Yes, she scooted out after Mother arrived."

"How are you?"

"Hungover after all that brandy you and Jane forced on me."

"Sorry."

"We've got the service planned for tomorrow. Peter made the arrangements. It will be in the Meeting House at four."

"We'll be there."

"Good."

A silence fell over the group, broken after several minutes by Demaris' quiet, gentle voice. "Had Harry been upset about anything lately? Anyone or anything happen out of the ordinary?"

"No, nothing like that. He's been excited about the weekend and unmasking Anne Greyson. He was trying to convince me to play the part, but I actually think he was looking forward to the moment of revelation."

"No odd phone calls? Visitors?"

"Not that I know about, but he kept the business side of things to himself. Liz Reynolds would know better than I. He went to Boston earlier in the week, but didn't seem upset or preoccupied when he returned. There was one funny thing."

"Oh?"

"He goes up to the library in Northport to do research. That librarian, Ms. Conlon, who's here for the weekend. She helps him, I think. He went last Tuesday and when he got back, he canceled our dinner plans and said he had to work."

"On?"

"He didn't say."

"Was that unusual, for him to cancel plans so abruptly?"

Bess gazed at him, eyes questioning. "A little, I guess, but sometimes things would come up."

"Like what?"

"Mostly things to do with his father. If he needed him, or wasn't feeling well."

Suddenly, he remembered the real reason for his visit. Sad eyes regarded her for a moment. He hated to speak knowing his words would shred the tiny thread of serenity she now possessed.

"Bess, about Mr. Winthrop."

"Oh,   no,   something's   happened   to   him.   Is   he—"
"He's all right, or was, last time I heard. No, it's Ralph Boardman. He's been murdered."

As Bess collapsed, fainting against her mother's shoulder, Pete caught her and prevented a crash to the floor. He then lifted her, carried her through to the study, and lay her on the couch.

Her mother bent over her, lightly patting her cheek. "Bess, sweetie? Please, darling, wake up."

Demaris went back to the kitchen, grabbed a clean washcloth and wet it. When he returned to the study, Bess' eyes were fluttering. "Here, dab her face with this."

"Should we call the doctor? She's never fainted in her life, that I know of."

"Has she eaten?"

"Just a few bites of dry toast."

"My guess is it's an empty stomach mixed with the brandy from last night, but we'll phone on our way out. Are you okay with her? Should we call Jane or someone from the village?"

"My dear Roger!" She started, then softened. "No, we'll be fine."

"We have to go. We'll ask the doc to stop by and I'll be back later. Try to keep her home, in bed."

The older woman nodded, and they turned to go.

"Roger?" Maggie Guilford whispered.

"Yes?"

"Who is Ralph Boardman?"

"A gardener and handyman on the Winthrop estate. He and his son live there, above the barn."

"Oh, dear," she said, turning back to find her daughter's eyes filled with tears.

Chapter 25

Harry Winthrop Senior looked as if he had shrunk to half his size. Slumped in an oversized armchair, his legs covered with an eiderdown lap quilt, he appeared to be drinking a snifter of brandy, a large one.

"Sorry, Lieutenant," he said, waving the snifter with quavering hand. "I have permission from my doctor, just one, to get me going."

Demaris took a seat beside him in a sturdy Windsor chair. "How are you holding up?"

"I'm alive, for the present. Let's leave it at that."

"I'm sorry about Ralph."

"He was a good man. Didn't deserve a fork in the back, nor did my son deserve an arrow in the chest. You're looking for a cowardly bastard, aren't you? First, he hides in the bushes and shoots my dear boy, then attacks poor Ralph from the rear. Probably figured he'd never have a chance with a frontal assault. Have you gotten anywhere with this?"

"Not yet, I'm 'fraid. It's our belief that Mr. Boardman may have seen the killer when he went to find Harry in the woods. Perhaps the jogger he mentioned to me. But, this may not be what happened at all. Did he say anything to you about seeing someone?"

"No, except the person in the running suit, but they're a dime a dozen over there by the school. Where Harry was running is a popular jogging trail, I understand."

Pete checked in on Molly Pierce and Helen Stevens, then returned to join the two men, notebook in hand. Demaris looked up and Pete shook his head. "Nothing about the jogger," he said, quietly, coming to stand five feet behind his boss.

"Aside from the fact that they lived in the same household and Ralph Boardman was your employee, did he and Harry have any other relationship?"

"Such as?"

"Would Boardman have helped with any of Harry's work? Errands? Driving him to Boston?"

"No, except the odd trip to the airport. They were friendly, of course. You know my son. He was naturally gregarious. Made friends easily. He and Ralph often shared a beer in the late afternoon before supper. Would sit out on the back terrace. Sometimes Charlie and I joined them, if the boy was around. They'd talk sports and what was happening around the farm or village. My son was a terrible gossip."

"When was the last time he drove Harry to the airport?"

"Only once, I think, when he went to New York on business. There may have been another time, but I can't recall. Helen or Molly may remember."

Heavy with sleep and sorrow, the old man's eyes were nearly closed now. The snifter tipped precariously in his quavering left hand and Demaris leaned forward, gently taking the glass and setting it on the table beside him.

"We'll let you rest now, Mr. Winthrop. I promise, you'll know as soon as we discover anything."

The man gave a crooked, half smile as his head dropped to his chest. "Get the housekeeper," Demaris whispered to Pete. "That position doesn't look comfortable or safe."

When Helen Stevens appeared, they said their goodbyes and headed out to the barn where her nephew was supervising the collecting of debris around the barn door.

"Anything, Brendan?"

"No, sir, not yet."

"Well, it's time to head into town anyway, for another meeting with the horde. All their whereabouts accounted for yesterday morning and last night?"

Dugan nodded. "Greta's got it all, boss. She's probably herding them together now."

"Okay, let's head into town. At some point, I want to talk to Charlie Boardman, but it can wait."

CHAPTER 26

When they were all gathered round the guest house table, Greta began.

"The ladies in the book club were playing cribbage until almost midnight. At least two of them were always together in the morning hours when Mr. Winthrop was shot."

"I doubt any of them is strong enough to drive a pitch fork straight through Ralph Boardman," Pete muttered. Always peevish when Greta was given more status than he, he squirmed in his seat and shuffled papers, his freckled cheeks flushed.

After a glance at his petulant second-in-command, Demaris waved a hand. "Greta, please go on."

"The librarian was in the parlor or her room during both times, but she may have taken a short walk."

"Again, I doubt Miss Marple could wield a pitchfork, much less a bow and arrow."

"Would you like to take over, Pete?" she asked, her expression impassive. "You've read these."

Dugan shrugged.

"Then there are the rest. Littlefield was all over the place, Hargreaves, the college roommate, too. That guy Stewart and his girlfriend were jogging in the morning and left dinner early for a stroll around the village. Wolfson, as you know, went on a bender, but he had time between dinner and his stint at the taproom to have driven out to the estate and killed Mr. Boardman. He was also out and about in the morning."

"Hiking," Demaris said, quietly.

"We did learn something about Hargreaves, sir," she said. "Actually, Brendan uncovered it in checking his background. Apparently, Professor Hargreaves is the faculty advisor for the college's archery club."

"Good work, Stevens," he said, smiling at the young officer, who blushed crimson.

"Amazing what a quick Internet search'll tell you, sir."

Greta grabbed another file folder. "We haven't even started on school people. We have a list. After this meeting, we'll start interviewing."

"What about the Reynolds woman? Her biceps were nothing to sneeze at," Demaris said, eying Pete before turning to Greta.

"She was supposedly power walking, then in her room making calls. As you know, she claims she was still in Boston when Harry died, but so far, no one can confirm when she left or arrived here."

"And she's staying at?"

"Do I look like I miss a workout, Officer Dugan?" Pete said, mimicking Liz Reynolds sultry voice. "Claims she can't be more than fifty yards from a gym. She's at the inn. Actually, it was kind of funny because I overheard her talking to some of the book club ladies, who are all at the B&B, and how they get free passes to the Harbor Gym while staying there. During one of her strolls along Main Street, she noticed the gym and I fear that's a step up from the two by four foot workout room in the inn's basement. Now, she has gym envy."

"All right, all right. Let's move on. This afternoon, you two start in on the school people. After we address the troops, I'll take Stevens over to talk with Arthur Burnham."

"Boss, I could come along with you and Stevens could go with Greta."

Ignoring his assistant, he continued, "Greta and Pete will chat with Stewart and the girlfriend after we break up and I'm going to grab Hargreaves and Wolfson."

"At the same time, sir?" Greta said meekly, afraid to get caught in the crossfire between her two superiors.

"No, we'll figure it out. You and Stevens head over to the inn. Pete, hold on a minute, will you? We'll be there in five minutes, Greta. Thanks."

Cheeks red, brow sweaty despite the guest house's damp chillness, Pete paced, head down. He reminded Demaris of himself eight months ago, and wondered again, if he had been a terrible role model for this young man he loved like a son. "Sit down, Pete, please?"

Dugan flopped on the loveseat. "This is bullshit. We, you and I, always work together. Greta does the legwork and coordinating with other people and I stay with you. Now, just because it concerns a certain someone, I've been demoted and banished from your interviews."

The older man sat silent for a few minutes, regarding his red-headed assistant. There was, of course, an element of truth to Pete's words. "You may be right. Not about the banishing part, but my decision has to do with focus. Mine."

"That's what I do, keep you focused!"

"Yes, you do, and I miss having you with me more than I can say. I depend upon you for everything, which is why I brought you with me to R.H.D. instead of leaving you here with Chief Wilbur."

'Then why?"

"You know me too well, my friend."

"That's right. That's exactly why I should be with you."

Demaris shook his head. "Okay, okay, I'm still in love with her, always have been, always will be. I was happy that she was happy with Harry Winthrop, but feelings are feelings."

"Are you telling me you're a suspect?"

"No, he irritated me, but I have to admit I kinda liked the guy, and he made her happy. Pete, I'm having this conversation now with the understanding that it will never happen again. Your mother henning is a distraction. A distraction we can ill afford on this one. Besides, with all the fricking suspects we're dredging up, I need you on the primary interviews. I have a handful of the others, but only one of you. Between you and Greta, you'll get the job done and done right. Stevens is a great kid, but he's what, two months out of the academy? He's better with me."

"But—"

"No more time for buts, my friend. You're still my right hand man and always will be, but I need you to go along with this, okay?"

"Yes, sir."

"Okay, let's go get 'em, partner."

They rose and he patted Dugan's shoulder. The other stiffened, then seemed to relax a little. "Okay, but if someone starts shooting at you, I'm coming back whether you like it or not."

CHAPTER 27

"About time you condescended to join us, Detective. I cut short an important call, hurried down here, and we've all been sitting around twiddling our thumbs."

Greta stepped forward. "It's Lieutenant Demaris, Mr. Littlefield, and since you've only just arrived, I don't think there's been time for thumb twiddling."

Her rebuke produced a soft smattering of twitters in the crowded parlor as many eyes turned to the impeccably dressed publisher now perched on a chair just inside the door. He looked much less comfortable without a sofa to lounge upon.

Demaris scanned the room and made eye contact with each person. Finally, he cleared his throat. "Thank you, everyone. We promise not to keep you long. It's a beautiful fall day and I'm sure you'd all like to enjoy it."

"Humph."

"Did you have something to contribute, Mr. Stewart?"

"No, I was simply agreeing with you. It would be nice to get out and enjoy the day and try to salvage something from this disaster of a weekend."

"Yes, well, let's get on, shall we?" He smiled at the disgruntled man, dressed as usual, in expensive jogging suit, a baseball cap resting in his lap. His lady friend, June Haglund, sat beside him on one of the stiff Victorian loveseats. She also wore jogging attire, pale blue with a blue floral scarf wrapped around her moppet of red curls. She fidgeted, hands in continual motion as she clasped and unclasped them. Poor woman, he mused, wondering if their "friendship" would survive the weekend or whether June would rush home and cancel her match.com membership forthwith.

"As I'm sure you've heard, there has been another death, or murder, I should say."

Claire Rubin nodded. "They told us at breakfast. Another member of the Winthrop household?"

"Yes, the gardener, Ralph Boardman. Did any of you know him?"

Blank stares and shaking heads answered him.

"Dad of my bartender, I understand," Boyle Wolfson muttered from the back of the room. "Poor kid." Wolfson looked surprisingly well considering his previous evening's bender.

"What do you mean, your bartender?" Liz Reynolds snapped, sitting up beside Tim Hargreaves on the room's other loveseat. "We all knew poor Charlie. Are you forgetting he served at Thursday's Reception?"

"Now, now, Liz, calm down," Hargreaves said, placing a protective hand on hers. "We're all a bit frayed this morning."

Demaris made a note to inquire how well the loveseat companions knew each other and went on. "If I could continue? My detectives have been making inquiries and have established the whereabouts of most of you. The ladies of the book club have moved as a group, or in pairs and threes for the times in question, and Ms. Conlon seems to have attached herself to one of these groups during the time of both murders. Therefore, you are all free to go home, unless there are some staying on for tomorrow's memorial service for Harry Winthrop. The time and place of Mr. Boardman's service have not, to my knowledge, been established."

"What about the rest of us?" Stewart said, waving his baseball cap.

"Let's see what today brings, shall we, Mr. Stewart? My detectives will interview you and Ms. Haglund in a few minutes. And, I would like a word with the three other gentlemen, Mr. Littlefield, Mr. Hargreaves, and Mr. Wolfson, if you don't mind?"

"As a matter of fact, I do mind," Littlefield said, standing to face him.

Instantly, Pete came between them. "Sit."

Littlefield sat.

"Are there questions before we break?"

"You didn't mention me, Lieutenant," said Liz Reynolds. "Of course, I'll be staying for dear Harry's funeral, but after that, am I free to return to Boston?"

"Let's wait and see where we are then. You are such a valuable source of information about Mr. Winthrop's business dealings, that it's helpful to have you here."

Hargreaves draped an arm around her shoulders, nodding. "That's true, sweetie." He turned to Demaris. "You cannot believe one of us had anything to do with these murders? Who are you looking at in the village? I'm sure there are plenty of people with far more reason to kill both men. I mean, no one here even knew the Boardman fellow."

Esther McPhee, one of the book club members raised her hand. "What if poor Ralph saw Harry's killer?"

"So you knew Mr. Boardman?"

"Only slightly. My husband, Lionel, had some business dealings with the elder Mr. Winthrop a few years ago. "Ralph would drive Harry Senior when he visited us."

"I see," Demaris said, eying Greta and Pete. There had been nothing in the interview notes about Mrs. McPhee's revelation. "Perhaps I could have a quick word now, after everyone disperses?"

She nodded and Demaris dismissed the assemblage asking Hargreaves, Wolfson, and Littlefield if they would meet him at the Tavern in a few minutes. Esther McPhee chatted with several members of the book group, then followed Demaris into the adjoining parlor.

When they were seated, he said, "Would you like something? Water? Tea?"

"Oh, no thank you, Lieutenant. The girls and I are having lunch at the Café. It's one of our favorite spots. We often hold book club meetings there."

"Best sandwiches in the county," he said, smiling at her. "But, don't tell Pop or Tilly I said that." Pop's Diner, the Corner Café, and the Tavern comprised the sum total of eating establishments in the village.

"Now, why don't you tell me about your husband's relationship with the Winthrops."

Barely five feet tall, Esther McPhee was what one would call a tidy dresser. Her beige wool slacks were perfectly tailored and matched her beige heathered sweater. Her blond hair had been styled in a tight pageboy that reminded him of a rugby helmet. He guessed her to be in her late fifties, early sixties. "They were friends and contemporaries, Lionel and Harry Senior. They went way back, way before my time. I'm Lionel's third wife, and there's a bit of an age gap between us. His previous wives are deceased."

"Are they still close friends?"

"I'm afraid not." Her blue eyes reflected what appeared to be genuine sadness at this development. "One of my husband's businesses was land development. He and Harry Senior invested in a large tract of land just north of Mattapoisett, where we live. My husband hoped to build an exclusive, one-of-a-kind enclave of luxury homes. Some of the properties had ocean views. It would have been lovely."

"But?"

"There were issues with the land. Liens, wetlands, various things. Harry felt they were insurmountable, Lionel did not. Harry sold his portion to another developer and before long the entire project collapsed. We lost almost everything."

"I'm sorry to hear that."

"They've not spoken since. I know Lionel misses his old friend, but he's still so angry and so proud. It wasn't Harry's fault, but Lionel felt abandoned nonetheless."

"Thank you, Ms. McPhee. Don't let us keep you from your lunch. Would you like Officer Stevens to walk you down to the Café?"

She blushed, eyes demure. "Oh, no thank you. I think I'm safe walking two blocks."

When the front door closed behind her, he turned to Stevens. "Let's head over. I'll take Hargreaves, then Wolfson. Let Littlefield cool his heels a while, the little twit."

CHAPTER 28

Tim Hargreaves appeared to have drenched himself in sandalwood, perhaps in hopes of attracting Ms. Reynolds. Demaris found it a welcome relief from the musty, damp smell of the guest house. Hargreaves had stopped off at the tap room to order and Demaris grabbed a water for himself. They now sat facing each other in the sitting alcove, in the small, uncomfortable, green canvas armchairs. Stevens sat in a straight back chair at the table behind them, notebook open, pencil poised. The recorder had already been switched on and placed on the coffee table between the men and Hargreaves had been read his rights.

"Well, that was fun. I'm grieving for one of my dearest friends and now I'm a suspect?"

"As Officer Stevens explained, it is standard procedure for all interviews in a murder case."

"I've seen the cop shows."

Ignoring the sarcasm, Demaris breathed deeply and began. "How long have you known Harry Winthrop, Mr. Hargreaves?"

"Tim, please, or you could call me 'Doc' like my students do. Can't quite bring themselves to be informal and use my first name."

"Is that unusual, that kind of informality?"

He shrugged. "Greenleaf's as elitist as the next place, I guess. One of my least favorite aspects of academia and all the professors pretending they're better, smarter, more learned than everyone else?"

"And, are they?"

His companion snorted. "Not that I've noticed. Anyway, I think you asked how long I've known Harr. We were roommates at Exeter so we go back a ways. We met freshman year, hit it off, and the rest is history."

"Strange that you hadn't yet met Ms. Dore."

"Haven't seen much of Harr since he came to Old Harbor. In fact, hadn't seen him since we parted after our last trip. One of the reasons I thought this murder weekend might be a hoot. Get to see my buddy and get reacquainted with Anne Greyson so to speak. She and I are good friends. Maybe I should take up mystery writing and carry on with the series? Wouldn't that send my department into spasms?"

"What is your area of expertise?"

"American literature, Hawthorne to Pynchon."

"Was Harry an English major?"

"Yup, damn smart, he was. Could have gone on as I did. Should have gone on as I did. He'd have made a great teacher."

"Was there tension between you the last time you parted company?"

The question, coming as it did out of the blue, flummoxed Hargreaves for an instant, but he recovered quickly. "Not on my end, no. But remember, he was still grieving for Stella."

"The first fiancée?"

"What a nightmare that was."

"Were you there the night she died?"

"Nope, on a semester abroad. I was in Sussex teaching. Would have come back for the wedding, had there been one. It was an anniversary party, as I recall. Bill and Lenore Jacobson's tenth, maybe? Bill was Harry's Harvard roommate. "

"How well did you know Stella Lang?"

"Only met her once. They came to England for the weekend. You can do that if you're filthy rich. Drove down from London and we had dinner in Brighton, the best vegetarian restaurant in the world. Harry and I have both shared that proclivity since college. Stella spent the evening moaning about wanting a good steak."

They were way off topic, but Demaris' curiosity was piqued. He set his water down and sat up. "What were your impressions of Ms. Lang?"

Hargreaves whistled, setting his empty beer stein on the table beside him. "Well, for starters, she was hands down one of the most beautiful women I've ever seen. The polar opposite of his current fiancée, in fact. A bit of an ice princess for my taste, but lovely. Have you seen photos?"

Demaris shook his head.

"Dark eyes, gorgeous blonde, delicate features, perfect body. Would have wooed her myself if she wasn't so smitten with Harr. Spent the evening draped all over him."

"Did you know Ralph Boardman?"

Lost in his reverie about Stella Lang, Hargreaves flinched at the abrupt change of subject. "No, as I told your detectives, I've never been to the Winthrop estate. Last time I saw the old man was on Beacon Hill, before the rest of the family was killed."

"Can you account for your whereabouts last night?"

"As I told your freckle-faced assistant, I had a quick beer at the Tavern after dinner, then took a walk around the village."

"You're at the inn, I believe?"

"Yes."

"What time did you get back there?"

"I haven't a clue. There was no one at the desk when I came in and I went straight to my room and graded a batch of papers, which put me right to sleep."

"What about the morning Harry Winthrop was killed? I believe you arrived the day before and attended the weekend's Welcome Reception?"

"I did, indeed. Was great to see Harry and meet Bess. Harry and I were actually going to jog together. He was a bit more serious runner than I am at present. Besides, I have a groin pull. He was going to do the campus loop and meet me on the village green and we'd do a mile or two together. When he didn't show up, I did a quick couple of miles on the road heading out of town, then came back to shower. Heard the news when the others did, at the B&B."

"I understand you are the faculty advisor for the Greenleaf Archery Club?"

Hargreaves leaned back, smiling. "I was wondering when you'd get to that."

"And?"

"And, what? Did you think I brought my bow and quiver with the intention of killing my best friend six weeks before his wedding? What possible motive would I have? I loved the guy. I'm sure your detectives are searching my room and car for evidence as we speak. As a matter of fact, I believe my archery bag is in my trunk. I keep it there. If the arrows are a match, I'd be very much surprised."

Hargreaves was flustered. Was it outrage or guilt? Demaris stared at him for a minute or two before speaking. "You seem to know Ms. Reynolds well."

"Not really, but our paths have crossed. She's worked for Harry for a long time. To my knowledge, only she and I, and maybe the old man, and fiancée knew the true identity of Anne Greyson."

Demaris turned to the young man behind him and raised an eye. Stevens closed and pocketed his notebook and stood. "Thank you, Mr. Hargreaves. You have been very helpful. I'm afraid we are going to have to ask you to remain in town for a few days. If this is a financial hardship, please let my detectives know."

"My reservations were for a week. I was planning to hang out with Harr and fiancé, have dinners at the estate, take some hikes. It's the college's fall break and I'd arranged to extend it a few days."

"Well, then, we'll know where to find you. Have you seen old Mr. Winthrop yet?"

"No, I didn't want to disturb him. Thought I'd touch base after the service and ask if he'd welcome a visit."

"He's quite frail."

"So I hear."

"Well, thank you. Officer Stevens will walk you back."

"I hardly need a babysitter, but fine. I'm assuming he's heading over to collect the next poor bastard."

The men were at the door and Stevens had opened it when Demaris said, "Oh, one more thing, Mr. Hargreaves, since you have your archery equipment with you, might we call upon you for a demonstration and perhaps, your expertise?"

"I live to serve, Lieutenant."

"Well, then, goodnight."

Cocky bastard, Demaris mused as the door closed behind them. Cocky, but was he a killer? He grabbed his cell phone and dialed Pete's number. When he reached voice mail, he said, "Pete, I need you and Greta to start digging into Harry Winthrop's past with Tim Hargreaves, their college days, travels, whatever. And dig up all you can on the first fiancée, Stella Lang."

He had barely clicked off his phone when Stevens appeared, Wolfson in tow.

CHAPTER 29

"I was crazy about her, Lieutenant. Half in love with her, in fact. Have you read Anne Greyson's work?"

"You mean Harry Winthrop's work. Light mysteries, I understand?"

"Mysteries that probed the depths of the human psyche. Ruth Rendell-like, only not quite so dark."

"I don't read a lot of mysteries, but I have read a few by Rendell. I wouldn't have guessed there were similarities between the two based on what I've heard of the Greyson books."

"That's because people don't go deep enough. They just don't get it."

"I imagine you were shocked to learn the truth about Ms. Greyson?"

"Horrified, betrayed, bereft would be more accurate. I've been trying for years to get her to my shop for a book signing. Mine's the largest mystery bookshop in New England, you know. It would have been a major coup to get Anne Greyson as she's so popular right now."

"To whom did you deal in trying to affect this coup?"

"That insufferable Reynolds woman. She serves as firewall between Anne and her public. Totally useless trying to go through the publishers or her. One of them is here, Mr. Slick, from the Littlefield Group. Amazing thing is, I don't think he knew about Anne's true identity until this weekend either. That's a pretty major cover-up for modern publishing, especially in the age of e-books when authors are on Facebook and Twitter every five minutes."

"And, Anne Greyson had no presence on social media?"

"Not a peep. Remarkable, really, considering how well she sold."

"I know my detectives had a brief chat with you, but can you please bring me up to speed about your whereabouts the morning of Mr. Winthrop's death?"

"Early morning I was nursing a hangover. Hadn't heard a peep about the Anne and Harry business. My girlfriend and I broke up this week. I haven't been at my best. Irony is, part of our break-up was because she was sick of my obsession with Anne Greyson. Pathetic, huh?"

"Is your girlfriend in the book business?"

Wolfson laughed, running his fingers through his dark, shoulder-length curls. "Hardly, one of us had to make money. She's a banker. Senior VP at Santander. Speaks Spanish, travels all over the world. Successful, in other words, unlike me saddled with a dying business."

"Even the largest mystery bookseller in New England is hurting, then?"

"We're holding on, but Sophie's well into the six figures now, while I barely draw a salary."

Demaris could sense there was something Wolfson wanted to say, so kept silent, not pressing. Maybe he was a grieving boyfriend and a time waster, but he decided to give him some time. "Can I get you anything? I'm having a water, but we have coffee, sodas?"

"No beer, I 'spose?" Demaris shook his head. "Water's fine, then."

Demaris sat, watching Wolfson fiddle with the label of his water bottle before finally unscrewing the cap. "It's a really small world, you know?"

"Oh, in what way?"

"Sophie actually knew Harry Winthrop. Met him in Madrid a few years ago before she and I started dating. I called her today to check in and she told me she'd heard about his murder. Was in the Globe, apparently, and the *Times*, and maybe every major newspaper."

Demaris nodded. "Yes, the Winthrops are a prominent family and then, there's Anne Greyson. How well did she know Mr. Winthrop?"

"They had a couple of dates, then his traveling buddy horned in. Was a bit of a tiff, apparently, both men after my Sophie. She's talented and beautiful, of course."

"And, did she tell you the outcome of this tiff?"

"She was in Madrid for the bank. When she left, that's the last she ever saw her two would-be suitors."

Small world, indeed, he mused, making a note to ask Hargreaves, whom he assumed was Lothario number two, about Madrid. "Let's get back to yesterday. So, you were nursing your hangover where?"

"First in my lumpy B&B bed, then I took a walk. Old Harbor Friends reminds me of my prep school days and it's always been meditative for me to walk a track oval. When I got back to the B&B news of Winthrop's demise had broken and the workshop group was in chaos. Couldn't tell if they were more upset about Winthrop's death or Anne Greyson's."

"I imagine you fell into the latter category?"

Wolfson shrugged, taking a swig of water. "Look, I barely knew the guy. I don't own a bow and arrow. I'm actually not a bad shot with a pistol. Lots of target practice. But, in my condition yesterday, I couldn't have hit the broad side of a barn with bullet or arrow."

"What were you wearing on your stroll through town?"

Wolfson stared, watery blue eyes questioning. "Old navy windpants and a ratty sweatshirt, why?"

"And, what did you do after dinner last night, before our encounter in the taproom?"

"You're asking because of that gardener, right? Never laid eyes on the man, wouldn't know him if I saw him. Never been near the Winthrop estate, wouldn't know how to get there."

"No GPS in your car, then?"

"Okay, okay, after dinner I took a walk through the village. Went about a half mile on the south road, then turned around and headed back. Stopped in at the Harbor Gym to ask about their hours today, then headed into the Tavern. Cute gal at Reception might remember me. I think her name was Barb."

"Well, thanks. We may have to ask you to stay around a few more days, but let's touch base tomorrow. Have you got someone to cover the shop?"

"I'll phone after this. Just another gazillion dollars of overtime to my worker bees. Maybe Allie, my manager, can fill in."

Demaris eyed Stevens and the two men disappeared, leaving him with more questions and no answers.

A few minutes later, Stevens returned alone to report that Carrion Littlefield had been taken ill and gone back to his room at the inn.

"Let's go, Brendan. Mr. Littlefield isn't getting off that easily."

CHAPTER 30

They stepped into the inn's front parlor where chaos reigned. A stretcher was headed up the stairs as Frip, the night manager wrung his hands. Several of the guests including Stewart and his date, were shouting at Pete and Greta, who stood guard at the foot of the stairs.

"What the hell is happening?" Demaris cried to no one in particular.

"Littlefield has a nut allergy. Apparently, he had a bowl of Tilly's Tavern stew and his throat closed up. Tilly claims there are no nut products in it, but he was clearly experiencing anaphylactic shock. He had an EpiPen and gave himself a shot, but doc wants him to go to the hospital to be sure."

"Where's the stew?"

"We bagged it and sent to Megan and the crew."

"Okay, okay, once they get him stabilized, I want to talk to Littlefield. For now, see that he gets off and come back to the guest house. Brendan, you accompany Mr. Littlefield in the ambulance and do not, under any circumstances, allow him out of your sight. If anyone at the hospital gives you a hard time, call me immediately."

"Yes, sir."

Stevens positioned himself at the front door just as the stretcher descended. Littlefield was awake, but groggy. Demaris raised his hand and the EMTs paused. "Mr. Littlefield, can you hear me?"

Pale and ghastly white, the patient nodded and his eyes fluttered open. "You're safe now. We have a police officer with you and we will be along directly." He nodded and the stretcher proceeded, Stevens following in its wake.

Demaris paced as he debriefed his detectives about the Wolfson and Hargreaves interviews. Greta and Pete shuffled papers, preparing for his questions.

"What'dya learn from Stewart?"

"Nothing, boss," Dugan said. "He was jogging yesterday morning, she stayed in the room. He was wearing a navy jogging suit. He said he ran around campus, but claims he didn't go in the woods. Too muddy. Saw a few students and might've passed a guy at some point, couldn't describe him. Guy's a prick. Can't see what June sees in him."

"What about last night?"

"She went back to the room with a headache and he took a drive."

"Oh?"

"Claims he headed south and then took the beach road and walked along the ocean at Wilkie's Point."

"Anyone vouch for that?"

"Nope."

"Okay, then he stays. I'd like to talk with her at some point, then I think we could probably let her go home. Did they come together?"

"Yup."

"Okay, well we'll get her back to New Hampshire somehow."

"She's from Newton actually," Greta said, flipping a page in her notebook.

"Newton, then." He looked from one to the other and realized they were all exhausted, especially Greta, who looked as if she hadn't slept in a week. Her hair, tangled and askew, stuck out at odd angles from a haphazard ponytail, her jeans were soiled with what looked like catsup and her gray sweater had several moth holes dotting its front.

"You two take a break. I'm gonna head to the hospital, then I'll be back. I still need to speak to the assistant headmaster, but not until after six tonight. You've got a lot of ground to cover with the others at the school, if you can find anyone today."

"I'll come with you, boss," Dugan said, reaching for his jacket.

"No need. Steven's there."

His assistant opened his mouth to argue, but then remained silent.

CHAPTER 31

While still pale, Carrion Littlefield was sitting up, chatting on his cell phone when Demaris walked in. Stevens had risen from his chair just outside the room and was on his heels. If he noticed his visitors, Littlefield gave no indication, but went right on talking.

A nurse popped her head in. "Are you family?"

"Police."

"He can be discharged. We're waiting on a prescription for him. New Epi and some antihistamines the doctor ordered, but he seems to be doing well."

"Mild reaction, then?"

"Seems so, but everyone reacts differently with nut allergies. He had apparently only taken a bite or two of his meal. Appeared to be concentrating more on the libations, if you ask me," she added, winking, then withdrawing.

Demaris came to stand over the bed, directly in the patient's line of vision. Littlefield waved a finger, then said to his caller, "Gotta go, Sam. Will phone later. Hope I'll be back tomorrow, but may be a few. Chow."

"How are you feeling, Mr. Littlefield?"

"Have you ever had anaphylactic shock, Detective?"

"No."

"Well, it's incredibly frightening, a true brush with death. And, in the aftermath, you feel like you've been run over by a bus."

"I'm sorry to hear that. Fortunately, you hadn't eaten too much of the stew, was it?"

"Just a bite, but that's all it takes. What idiot puts peanut butter in stew? I didn't like the taste and sent it straight back to the kitchen. Thank God."

"Did you order something else?"

"I asked for a Cobb salad. One of the others had ordered one and it looked marginally palatable. Unfortunately, I felt ill before it was served. Just as well. The food in this rinky dinky town is atrocious."

"Whom were you dining with?"

"I was attempting to dine alone, but was instantly besieged by the workshop people still trying to go on with their getaway as if the main attraction wasn't cold on a gurney somewhere. Idiots, if you ask me."

"And the names of these optimists?"

"That hideous man with the blonde bobble-headed girlfriend, always dressed in matching jogging suits. They joined us after their interrogation. Liz Reynolds and Hargreaves were there until you yanked him away for his inquisition. Liz invited that mousy librarian to join us, although I cannot imagine why. Boring doesn't begin to describe the woman. No wonder she was mooning over darling Harry."

"I admire your boundless compassion, Mr. Littlefield."

"Listen, Detective, I publish hundreds of authors. Yes, Anne Greyson was a good, steady seller, but I didn't know her, never met her and I'm not inclined to weep in my soup over a little lost revenue."

"Are you feeling up to a few questions about the past few days?"

"Absolutely. I'll be out of this dump in a few minutes anyway, soon as they bring me my clothes and a new Epi. Have you seen the doctors? They look like they're ten and attended medical school on a Caribbean vacation."

"The medical care is actually quite good here, but let's get on with this so you can get dressed and be on your way, shall we? Would it be all right if Officer Stevens takes a photo? You arrived late and were not included in the group shot they took at Thursday night's Reception."

"Well, since he read me my rights five minutes ago and has his recorder ready, I assume the indignity of having a photo in my hospital bed won't kill me. This, after I informed you about my arrival time Friday, which was long after one of my best-selling authors was murdered."

"Yes, well, as I'm sure Officer Stevens told you, this is routine procedure for anyone questioned in a homicide investigation."

"Fine, fire away!" He sat up, brushed locks of dark hair from his forehead and grimaced as Stevens snapped two shots with his iPhone. He reminded Demaris of a baby robin, thin arms protruding from the cavernous sleeves of his lime green Johnny. Lime was not his color.

"Now then, I know you arrived at noon, but I'm afraid no one can verify this. Did you stop for gas, perhaps? At a convenience store along the way? Or maybe run an errand while you were still in the city?"

"No, nothing like that. I did get gas, but only after I'd driven into Hicksville and realized the tank was nearly empty. I went back out to Route Six to a station I'd passed on my way in."

"Oh, and what time was that?"

"Not sure, but I came straight from there to the B&B for that hideous brunch where I learned about Harry, aka Anne's death. Didn't even stop to check in at the inn. Wish I'd driven right back out of town. I'd be soaking in my Jacuzzi right now instead of talking to you."

The entire time Littlefield spoke, he waved one arm, then the other in extravagant gestures, apparently meant to underscore his fascinating conversation. Demaris caught Stevens out of the corner of his eye trying to follow the man's movements and wondered if he might end up hypnotized.

"What about Ralph Boardman? Did you know him?"

The abrupt change in topic brought the patient to stillness and he settled his long fingers into his lap, grabbing hold of a fold of sheet. "Never heard of him. The handyman, right?"

"Are you acquainted with the Winthrops, Mr. Littlefield?"

"Only the name. If you live on Beacon Hill, you've heard the name Harry Winthrop, the senior. Never met the man, or his son though. Family's been marked with tragedy. The accident that killed his wife and daughter was in the papers for weeks."

"And, where were you after dinner last night?"

"As I told your officers, I went for a walk. After enduring incredibly mind-numbing conversation for over two hours, I'd had enough."

"A long walk?"

"Not particularly."

"Anyone see you?"

"No, not that I remember. It was night and this place seems to close up at around five right after the early bird specials end."

"So you've been in the dark about Anne Greyson all the years you have been publishing the books?"

"That would be correct. All our dealings have been electronic. On the rare occasion when I've called the office, I've spoken to the Reynolds woman."

"Were you shocked to learn that Anne was a male?"

"Detective, nothing shocks me in this business."

"It's Lieutenant," Stevens said, in a quiet voice.

"You're a lieutenant?" Littlefield said to the junior officer. "You look like you just graduated from elementary school."

Stevens opened his mouth, but Demaris beat him to it. "He means me, Mr. Littlefield. I think we're done here. I'm going to have to ask you to remain in Old Harbor for at least a day or two."

"Well, I'm going to the funeral, of course. Are you saying I can't leave tomorrow night?"

"Perhaps not. We may need your assistance and will want to ask you some follow-up questions in person. Ah, here's the nurse with your things. Officer Stevens will drive you back to town. Take care."

Before Littlefield could utter a syllable, Demaris disappeared, leaving him slack-jawed and staring from Stevens to the nurse.

Pete and Greta were just leaving the guest house when he returned.

"How'd you make out with Littlefield?" she said.

"He's a pain in the ass, but he doesn't seem any worse for the wear after his brush with death. Says he got gas on Route Six, just out of town. Check out the time, will you? I've told him that we might need the pleasure of his obnoxious company for a few more days. Where are you headed?"

"We caught the Upper School Head, Todd Bridgham, and he's agreed to talk to us," Pete said. "Couple of the ladies, too. That Nettleman woman and Kitty Bigalow. Remember them?"

"Unfortunately, yes. Good luck with those two. I'm going to head to the Tavern to speak to Tilly and get something to eat. Then, I'm going to shut my eyes in this chair for fifteen minutes."

"By the way, boss," he added, as he held the door for Greta. "Tilly said no way she put any peanut butter or any kind of nuts in the stew."

"I was afraid of that. See you in a few."

Demaris closed his eyes, not waiting for the door to shut behind them.

CHAPTER 32

Midafternoon, the Tavern was deserted. One of the cleaning staff told him Rachel, Tilly's partner and manager had gone home to their farmhouse at the edge of the village for a short nap. Demaris found Tilly on a stool chopping onions in the modern commercial kitchen. She wore safety goggles smudged with grease, which did not seem to be helping as tears flowed down her freckled cheeks.

"Hello, handsome." She removed the goggles, wiped her eyes and grinned. At six feet, she towered over him. "Won't hug you or you'll be covered in crap. You'd think after twenty years in the business, I'd be immune to onions. Kids usually do 'em, but I gave 'em a short break before I realized that we had to throw out all that blasted stew and start over." She wiped tears from her eyes and gestured for him to join her at an ancient butcher block table near the back door.

"Want anything? Drink? You hungry?"

"Thanks, I'm fine. How are you, Till?"

"I've been better. Not every day that a customer, even a little twit like that one, keels over in my restaurant. Rachel had to take four Xanax and go home. We'll never rouse her for the dinner crowd. I've had to call for reinforcements. We're all set, just a pain. So, how's my favorite top cop?"

"I've had better days."

He smiled at his old friend. Tilly was his brother Mike's age, two years younger than he. They had gone through school together, until college when she had headed off to culinary school and Roger to the Marines and his on-again, off- again relationship with Rhode Island School of Design.

Flecks of what looked like whipping cream dotted the edges and top of Tilly's ubiquitous hairnet, worn to contain her wiry, unruly curls, which were now salt-and-pepper like his own. "So what about the stew?"

"Roger, I haven't a clue. There were no nuts in it, I swear. Or if there were, I did not put them there. Are you having it tested?" He nodded. "Well, does that mean we'll be liable in some way? If Mr. Littlefield does not recover?"

"Mr. Littlefield is just fine. Sorry, I should have said that straight off. I'm no expert, but it looked like a very mild reaction."

"I understand he only had one bite?"

"Yes, he said he didn't like the taste and sent his bowl straight back and ordered a salad. We were just making it up when he apparently left, saying he felt unwell."

"What happened to his bowl?"

"Well, that's a bit of a problem. Charlie Boardman's Border Collie was tied up on the porch and he gave it to him. Chomps licked the bowl clean and it went into the dishwasher, I'm 'fraid. We didn't know, you see, until they came back from the inn looking for the stew. When Littlefield left, he was complaining, but nothing serious."

"I understand he consumed several glasses of wine?"

"Yes, all the while complaining about our poor selection."

"Who had access to the stew?"

"All of us, the kitchen staff. That's Billy, Wendy, and Sid today. And, of course Rachel. Charlie Boardman was in and out. I told him not to come at all, but I don't think the poor kid knows what to do with himself. After morning prep, Sid took over tending bar. They'll all be back soon. They're good kids. I can't imagine one of them mucking with my recipe. I was in the kitchen the entire day except when I ran down to the bakery to get more baguettes."

"What time was that?"

"Just after noon, I think."

"Okay, thanks, Till. I'll send Pete or Greta back to talk to the staff in a bit. We'll try not to interfere with dinner too much."

As if on cue, the three young workers along with Charlie Boardman, pushed open the back door. All appeared to be in their twenties, two of the guys were in jeans and tee shirts, and Charlie was dressed in black pants and an Oxford shirt, a bow tie at his neck. The young woman, Wendy, he assumed, wore black wool slacks, and a soft black sweater with plunging V-neck and heels, her dark hair swept up in a chignon.

"'Bout time. Wendy, you're out front, Sid behind the bar, and Billy, it's just you and me tonight, buddy. If Rachel makes a miraculous appearance, Wendy can rejoin us. Let's pray for a slow Sunday night. Boardman, didn't I tell you not to come back?"

"Don't send me home, Till. I need the money and I don't feel like sitting around with my uncle and aunt, okay?"

"Fine, get out there. Sid, you stay with Billy and me. She turned and winked at Demaris. "See you around, handsome."

He nodded and slipped out the door leading to the dining room just as Bess, Jane, and Maggie Guilford came through the front door. Maggie waved as she shooed her companions to a table by the window.

"Why, Lieutenant, how fortuitous! Are you here for tea? Please join us."

"Thanks, Ms. Guilford, but I'm just on my way out." He held the chair for her then turned to her daughter. "How are you?"

"Okay," she said softly.

"Any news?" Jane asked.

"Not yet. We had a minor kerfuffle this afternoon with one of the weekend people experiencing an allergic reaction."

"Who?" Bess cried, rising half out of her seat.

"Carrion Littlefield, the publisher. Not to worry, he's fine. Has a nut allergy and somehow ingested nuts in something."

"How awful, poor man." As she spoke, Bess wiped imaginary tendrils of hair from her cheeks.

"Roger, dear, please let's not get maudlin. This outing is to cheer Bess up. Help take her mind off things."

Good luck with that, he thought, reaching down to cover her hands, bringing them to stillness.

"Littlefield really is fine. Not to worry. Have a nice tea, ladies."

After returning to the guest house, he phoned Pete and told him to interview the kitchen staff and Charlie about the stew. Then, he clicked off his phone and sat on one of rooms lumpy upholstered chairs, closing his eyes. His intention was to meditate, but if sleep overtook him, so be it.

CHAPTER 33

Tilly placed a tray of small sandwiches, scones, and pots of tea in front of Bess and her companions, then excused herself to take orders from two adjoining tables. Pad and pencil poised, she failed to hear the order as the front door opened and a woman and small boy stepped in.

"Excuse me a minute, folks."

Tilly stepping back and headed for the pair. Backs to the door, Bess and Jane had observed the Tavern owner's odd behavior and turned in time to see Tilly greet Mary Demaris.

After embracing, they spoke in whispers for several minutes. They overheard Tilly say, "Of course, he can keep the guys and me company in the kitchen. May even put him to work." The child turned and followed the strange woman, who towered over him like a massive redwood. It was then that they caught a glimpse of him. About five or six years old, he was neatly dressed in a navy sweater and what looked like brand new, pressed khaki pants.

"Oh, my Lord," Jane whispered, as Maggie Guilford turned to see what they were gaping at. "He's a miniature of Roger."

"How is that possible?" Bess' mother asked as Tilly and the child disappeared through the kitchen door.

So rapt were they in their observations of the child that they failed to see Mary until she stood by the table. "Hello, Bess." The three jumped. "Sorry to startle you. It's been a while."

"Mary, hello." Bess hopped up and came around to hug the other woman. "So nice to see you. Sorry we were gaping."

"He's a clone of his dad, isn't he?"

She had removed her raincoat and draped it over her arm. Her dark brown shoulder-length hair was fashionably styled in a loose, pageboy, not a hint of gray . She wore a plaid skirt and navy sweater with sensible black flats. A plain sort of woman, but not unattractive.

"I never knew you had, I mean, I remember your daughter. She must be?"

"Ten, Terry's ten and Owen, whom you just saw is five."

"Roger never said, I mean, not that I asked, but—"

"He doesn't know about Owen, Bess."

"Jeez, Louise," Jane said.

"Yes." Mary said, quietly.

Mouth agape, Bess gazed at Mary Demaris. "Oh, I'm sorry, where are my manners? I don't know whether you remember my mom, Maggie Guilford? And Jane Fellows? Jane is my colleague at Old Harbor."

Jane nodded, but remained silent, lost in thought about Roger Demaris and the son whose first five years of life were unknown to his dad.

"Hello, Mrs. Guilford, haven't seen you since high school."

"Lovely to see you, dear. Your little boy is adorable."

"He's a good boy. I understood from Pete that Roger was here?"

"He just left a few minutes ago. I'm surprised Pete didn't come back with you."

"Believe me, he wanted to, but I asked him not to. Some things never change."

"Would you like to join us?" Bess asked. "We have plenty."

"No, thanks. I'll head over to the guest house now, before the others return. I fear it will be a bit of a shock for him. I was pregnant when we split up, you see. I never told him."

"My, dear woman," Maggie said. "You mean to tell us that he's had a son he didn't know about for five years?"

"I've got to go."

Mary Demaris took a step back, just as Bess murmured, "Poor Roger" and in those words betrayed the depth of her feelings for the woman's ex-husband. This realization was not lost on any of her companions.

"Yes, poor Roger," Mary said softly and without another word, turned away.

Chapter 34

The door opened and closed before Demaris stirred, stretched, and took one last mindful breath. He opened his eyes expecting to spy his team, or at least one of them. "Mary? What in the world?"

He stood.

"Hello, Roger."

She paused in the circle of silence, beige raincoat hanging on her diminutive frame like a cloak. She looked much the same as she had the last time he had seen her, nary a wrinkle on the smooth olive skin. Demaris shook himself and came forward to embrace her. She returned his hug stiffly, then immediately stepped back as soon as he released her.

"Have you a few minutes?"

"Of course, come in," he said, helping her with her coat. "Can I get you a soda? Water? Tea or coffee?"

"No, thanks, I'm fine. I think we should sit though."

"Of course, here." He indicated the loveseat and brought one of ladder-back chairs to sit in front of her. "Is anything wrong?"

"No, but I have something to tell you."

He smiled, waiting for her to continue.

"I'm glad to see that your calmness has stayed with you, since I saw you in June."

"That's what a heart attack and months of mindfulness meditation training will do for an angry middle-aged guy."

"Well, I'm glad for you and hope what I tell you won't destroy your calm."

"I dare say, I'll cope." He smiled again, waiting. "What's wrong, Mary?"

"Nothing. I've come to tell you that, well, that you have a…Roger, you have a son. Owen, he's five years old and he wants to meet you."

His chest constricted, the wind knocked out of him. As he struggled to catch his breath, he endeavored to comprehend what she was saying. "Excuse me?"

"I was pregnant when we split. When I came back for court, it was almost a year later. He'd been born and stayed with my sister when I came with Terry."

"Why?"

"I thought it'd be less complicated. Roger, I don't expect you to understand, but I had to make a clean break."

"Less complicated for whom? Jesus Christ, Mary! You've kept Terry from me except for the occasional visit even though you know I miss her like crazy. She barely knows me and now I find out I have another child, who doesn't know me at all?"

"I had to get out of this place. I couldn't live another minute watching you moon over Bess Guilford."

"Here we go, still obsessing about Bess."

"Do you deny it? Even after she was happily married, you were still crazy in love with her. When her husband died, I figured it was only a matter of time before you two would get together. I didn't want my kids raised by her, even part-time."

He took a deep breath, and reached forward to take her hands. "Bess is not the enemy, Mary. Never has been, never will be. It's been ten years since Mac died. Did you see us riding off into the sunset? She was engaged to be married in six weeks. Nice guy."

"I heard about the murder. How tragic."

"Yes, it is."

"Did she call you in? I mean, this isn't your territory anymore."

"Actually, it was her future father-in-law, Harry Winthrop Senior."

"I see. Well, I've left Owen with Tilly. Could I bring him over to meet you?"

"Of course, I'll come with you."

"No, Roger, please stay here. I don't want your meeting to happen with an audience. Your old girlfriend, her mom, and a friend are over there having tea, and the taproom was filling up when I left."

"Okay, whatever you want."

He retrieved her coat and helped her into it.

CHAPTER 35

He elected to sit and breathe slowly and so was still sitting when the door opened again and she reappeared, a dark-haired child just behind her. For an instant, Roger Demaris imagined he was looking in a mirror, a faraway mirror where he had grown very small.

"Here's Owen, then."

Before he could rise or utter a word, the boy crossed the room, sat on his lap, curled up, and put his head on his father's shoulder. Of all the scenarios Demaris could have imagined, this was not one of them. Surprised and pleased, he folded him in an embrace. "Hello, son."

When he looked up, Mary was dry-eyed, dispassionate, as if she were watching a dull television program.

"Might you have time to take us to dinner? We're staying in Northport. Maybe we could go out there? We leave in the morning."

"Are you at a hotel?"

"Nancy Parker's." Nancy was one of Mary's closest friends. They had gone to school together, gotten married the same year, and divorced within six months of each other.

He looked down at the child, smiling and patting his head. "We could go to the Grille? What do you like to eat, Owen?"

Owen shrugged, but remained silent.

At that moment, the guest house door swung open and Pete, Greta, and Stevens burst in, chattering away. When Pete spied Mary, then the boy on his boss' lap, he stopped midsentence. Stevens, who had witnessed Dugan's earlier encounter with Mary Demaris, looked from Pete to his superior and appeared ready to dive for cover. Greta remained impassive, quietly observing.

"How'd you three make out?" Demaris said quietly, acting for all the world as if his diminutive twin was not sitting on his lap.

Greta stepped away from Pete who appeared to be frozen just inside the door. "Not much to report, sir. School people checked out, but we think the assistant head and former head are worth a little more digging. Motives are a bit fuzzy though. You're talking to Burnham, right?" He nodded. "The notes are here. I'll copy them for you. Megan called. No nuts in the stew, at least the samples we took from the kitchen. As you know, Littlefield's bowl was taken back to the kitchen and given to Charlie's dog. The creature had no ill effects that we know of."

"What about Stewart and his friend?"

"He's a miserable human being," Pete said, finding his voice at last. "Whereabouts for both events sketchy, but no motive we could find. His lady friend appears to have spent most of the weekend in her room or the inn's spa."Staying away from him, no doubt, Demaris mused. 'Thanks, we'll catch up later. This is my son, Owen. Owen, these are my coworkers, Pete, Greta, and Brendan."

The three came forward and shook the child's hand, smiling and saying their hellos.

"Greta and Brendan, this is Owen's mother, Mary Demaris. I don't believe you've met?"

"Hello, very nice to meet you," Greta said, moving to shake her hand.

After shaking Greta's then Stevens' hands, Mary turned to him. "Roger, you're in the middle of this. We'll leave you to it."

Still seated, he said, "Can you three give us a minute?"

Unsure of where to go, the three tacitly decided outdoors was best and stepped out, closing the door.

"Come on, Owie, here's your coat. Your dad's busy and we should get back to Aunt Nancy's."

The boy stood, looking from one to the other of his parents. "I want to stay here," he said firmly, voice high-pitched as he planted himself alongside his father.

Demaris sat on the coffee table and brought himself close to the boy's eye level. "Your mom's right, son. I am in the middle of something, but we can still have dinner tonight. Would that be okay?" The child nodded and accepted his jacket from his mother.

He turned to Mary. "I have a short interview to do, then I'll head right up and meet you either at Nancy's or the restaurant?" "The restaurant would probably be best," she said, quietly. "Come on, Owie."

"Can I stay and ride up with you?" Icy blue eyes stared at him. Again, Demaris felt as if he were staring into a strange, size-altering mirror. He looked up at her, not wanting to overstep.

"That's up to you, Roger, but I don't want him at some grisly crime scene." "It's just a quick interview at someone's home. Stevens will be with me and I'm sure he and Owen could wait in another room. We won't be long."

"Fine." Visibly displeased, she seemed unwilling to fight with the child.

This trip had clearly not been her idea nor her choice. Either their son had incredible powers of persuasion or there was something else afoot.

She shrugged into her coat and turned to her ex-husband. "I'll make a reservation for seven at the Grille, but why don't you call when you're on your way to Northport. The Grille is five minutes from Nancy's condo."

"Sounds like a plan."

"Owie, be good and stay out of your father's way, understand?"

He nodded, and smiled the first smile Demaris had seen. Like his father, the smile completely transformed his face from a solemn mask to one of warmth and gentleness. It was an expression Mary had glimpsed many times over the five years of her son's life, but rarely in her marriage to his father. Roger had reserved his infrequent smiles for the love of his life, Bess Guilford, and now, it appeared, for his son.

CHAPTER 36

After leaving Owen with Stevens in the head of school's kitchen, Demaris followed Arthur Burnham to the house's study, where they sat surrounded by bookcases. The room was furnished in leather sofas, soft, exquisitely upholstered couches and chairs, and a priceless Aubusson rug on the wide plank floor. A massive entertainment center dominated one wall and another wall of windows overlooked the sweeping lawn and school main entrance.

"Isn't it a little unusual for you to move into the Head's home for such a short period of time, Mr. Burnham?"

"Not really. Pru and I thought the house should stay open and available to the community. My apartment is being renovated and has no space for gatherings. Many school events happen here. Seemed to make the most sense."

"So, how well did you know Harry Winthrop?"

"Not well, I'm afraid. I've seen him a number of times at school functions, of course, because of his association with Bess Dore."

Demaris held a notepad and had started the recorder. He wondered how Stevens and Owen were getting on. Lana Wilkins, the girlfriend, was nowhere to be seen. When they arrived, Burnham had blustered a bit about the Sunday evening intrusion and asked why they had not scheduled something with his assistant, Becky, on Monday as suggested. Demaris had apologized and offered no explanation, but promised to be brief. Now that they were settled, his host seemed more relaxed and cordial.

"Never met him prior to coming to Old Harbor?"

He shook his head. "Met the father several times, but young Harry was always traveling somewhere."

"What was your impression of Mr. Winthrop the younger?"

"Nice enough fellow. Enthusiastic. Jumped right into life in the village, I hear, although being so new myself, I have no basis for comparison."

"Was he close to anyone at the school besides Bess, I mean, Ms. Dore?"

"Not that I'm aware of. Seemed pretty chummy with the Thurberts, but I haven't a clue if they socialized or not."

"To your knowledge, did anyone on campus see anything the morning Harry was killed?"

"Absolutely not. Well, what I meant to say is -- not that anyone's informed me. I jog that trail almost every day. Horrible tragedy."

"Were you running that morning?"

"I took a short run, but used the track and stayed out of the woods. Too muddy after the rain and I had to be quick because Lana wanted to go to breakfast. She came down Thursday night, took the day off on Friday, in fact. So I wanted to spend time with her before leaving for work."

"I see. What about Ralph Boardman? Did you know him well?"

"Not at all. I did see him occasionally when I visited Mr. Winthrop Senior, but aside from a nod or hello, never even had a conversation with the man. And, if you're going to ask, I spent the evening with Lana. Was called to one of the dorms by Joan Nettleman for a small crisis, which was over by the time I arrived."

"What time was that?"

"About nine o'clock, I think."

"What was the crisis?"

"One of the boarders was missing and none of her friends knew where she was. They were a bit hysterical, especially since the young woman in question had left her cell phone in her room."

"And, where had she been?"

"She apparently has a new boyfriend whose name she would not divulge. I expect he's a local boy. She said they were driving around talking. I'm sure you can decipher the code there."

"I'll need her name."

"Is that necessary?"

"Yes, if they were riding around, or even parked somewhere, they might have seen something."

"Rebecca Rollins, Becca. She's a senior. Her father is the school's archivist."

"I didn't know Becca was a boarder?"

"You know her then?"

"Just from her mother's bookshop. I've watched her grow up."

Clarice Wills, Becca's mom, ran the village's small bookshop, which had an eclectic mix of fiction and nonfiction, the latter mostly books of local interest. She also carried used books, which patrons were free to borrow and return as they wished. The shop had a small parlor with tattered, but comfortable easy chairs. Readers could pour themselves a mug of coffee or tea and relax with a book. In earlier years, one would often find Becca Rollins stretched out on the floor working a puzzle or playing hide and seek with a friend in the stacks. When he worked in town, Demaris often stopped in at the end of the day or over lunch, the shop's musty warmth a welcome change from the station.

"Then you know the parents are divorced. Very nasty, as I understand it. He's on his second marriage, which I understand is also on the rocks. Custody disputes ferocious. Parents agreed she would be better off boarding than residing in either home. Unfortunately, I know how toxic such environments can be. My ex-wife was very unbalanced after our separation. My kids are grown now, but they went through hell for a couple of years."

Demaris was tempted to ask more about this new bit of unsolicited information, but decided to stick to the matters at hand. "We'll need to talk with Ms. Rollins. When would be best, do you think?"

"She's one of our field hockey stars. Right wing. She has classes, then practice or a game every day. I hate to have her pulled from class, but the students' lunch period is noon to one. Perhaps you could catch her then, or at practice? They don't have a game until Thursday."

"I understand that last summer, shortly after you arrived on campus, you made romantic overtures to Bess Dore?"

Burnham blanched. "Excuse me? Where on earth did you hear such nonsense?"

"From several sources, actually, including Bess herself."

"Well, I may have asked if she'd like to have lunch or dinner, but I was endeavoring to get to know all my staff."

"I see. What I've heard was more flirtatious in nature, not simply a friendly get-to-know-you type thing."

"Well, what you've heard is preposterous and untrue. I cannot imagine Bess saying something like that either."

"She didn't, but she did tell you she was involved with Harry Winthrop, who is now dead."

"I object to your tone and your insinuation, Lieutenant. Bess is one of our finest teachers. We have a professional relationship and nothing more. I am very involved with Lana and was pleased and happy to learn of Bess' engagement. Now, if there's nothing else, I have to change. Lana should be back from the gym any minute and we've got plans."

As Demaris rose, he noticed the assistant headmaster's hand shook as he set down his glass of water. He excused himself and found Stevens and Owen engaged in an exaggerated arm wrestling contest, which his son appeared to be winning. They said their goodbyes at the door. After instructing Stevens to check in with Becca Rollins and Joan Nettleman about Burnham's evening trip to the dorm, he and Owen walked hand in hand down the hill to Demaris' jeep in the parking lot just inside the campus gates.

CHAPTER 37

"Well, almost five, Owen, I'm very glad to meet you."

He gazed at the boy through the rear view mirror, his eyes warm with a smile. With no car seat, his mother had insisted that Owen sit in the back seat of the SUV.

"Yes, sir," he replied in a reedy soft voice.

Demaris' chest constricted with sadness at the loss of five years with this precious boy.

"No need for sir, son. If you're not ready for Father or Dad, you can call me Roger."

"Do you like being a policeman?"

"Sometimes. Most of the time. Not at this moment 'cause I'd like to spend more time with you, but it's a good job."

"What do you like?"

Demaris looked in the mirror and found eyes staring hard, curiosity and eagerness shining in their deep blue depths in the rosy twilight. "I enjoy working with young people. I have a great team. I also like puzzles, trying to piece things together, to read people and figure out what they're not saying. Keeps this old bachelor busy." And, if we're lucky, we uncover evil and bring cowardly monsters to justice.

"Do you have a gun?"

"Sometimes, yes. Not tonight."

"Do you get scared?"

"Can't do this job if you're not scared once in a while."

The boy sat silent for a few moments until Demaris asked, "What about you? What'd you like to do? Do you play sports?"

"I'm not very good. I hate P.E. I like reading and art."

There was that pain again, the loss of time, time when he could have shared his passion for painting with his child. He wished they were staying longer and he could drive Owen to his house, to show him the studio he shared with no one. "You sound like me. I wasn't great at sports, although I did play in high school. I loved to draw and paint, though. Art and recess were my favorite subjects."

"Mom told me."

As they drove up and parked in the restaurant lot, he asked, "Has your mom told you much about me?"

"When I ask, she tells me things. And, I have my album. It has pictures of you, Terry, and Grandma and Grandpa. One of Uncle Mike, too. Does he live near here?"

"Couple of hours away in Connecticut."

"Is he a policeman, too?"

Demaris chuckled as they walked toward the Grille's entry. "No, Mike's a lawyer. Makes tons of money and lives in a mansion."

"He has kids, doesn't he?"

"Four, your cousins. Little Mike is about your age, come to think of it."

"There you are," she called, opening the door. "I was beginning to worry."

"Mary, I'm sorry. We got to talking and I forgot to call."

"Mom, can we come back so I can meet my cousins?"

"Someday, sweetie. Let's eat, I'm starved."

Now that he had broken his silence, Owen chattered happily all through dinner, asking about police work, telling his father about school and his various projects that were underway in their craft room. Mary watched them, marveling as she had for five years at the resemblance. It went beyond the physical to gestures and body language, to the twinkling in their blue eyes when something excited them. She felt suddenly old and sad. Even if she couldn't bear to see Roger, it had not been right to keep father and son apart.

They had just ordered dessert when Demaris' phone buzzed. He excused himself and stepped outside the restaurant into the cool night air. "What's up, Pete?"

"Sorry to bother you, boss, but we have a situation here."

"What's going on?"

"Didn't want to call earlier 'cause I was afraid you'd cancel your dinner, but Hargreaves has been nothing but a nuisance all day. He's been phoning old man Winthrop and Ms. Dore, asking to stop by. Then, he actually did drop in on both of them. Helen Stevens wouldn't let him past the front door and Bess and her mom were driving off when he arrived."

"Did you speak to him?"

"We were looking for him when Tilly called. Hargreaves and that idiot Stewart got into a fistfight at the Tavern, egged on we understand, by Littlefield and Wolfson. Our friendly bookseller's plastered again."

"What in the hell were they fighting about?"

"Apparently each claimed to know the Winthrops intimately and were wondering aloud if they should speak at the service."

"Jesus Christ. Don't they know it's a Meeting for Worship and anyone can speak?"

"Yes, according to some of the book group ladies who observed the whole thing, they were arguing about whether it was appropriate for just anyone to speak. They were all half in the bag."

"What about Littlefield and Wolfson? What was their role?"

"Since neither of them knew Harry Winthrop personally, they decided to referee and got the other bozos going with their bragging about how well they knew the Winthrop family."

"But, Stewart didn't, did he?"

"Claims they go back to Maine days, when both his family and theirs summered in Bar Harbor."

"I see and why this is the first we've heard of it? Where are they now?"

"Made a huge mess of the taproom. Broken dishes, food everywhere. Tilly called the cops and the local guys tossed Hargreaves and Stewart in cells, waiting to see what you want to do with them."

"Leave 'em. I'll be back in an hour or two. Should've tossed those twits Littlefield and Wolfson in with 'em."

"They're back in their rooms. Stevens told 'em to stay put."

"Okay, thanks, Pete. I'll see you in a few."

He rejoined Mary and Owen just as their sundaes arrived.

After dessert, he paid the check and walked them to Nancy's car. "I'm sorry I have to go, and I'm even sorrier that you can't stay longer. When will you be back?"

"I was thinking Thanksgiving? Maybe Terry, Owen, and I could come back?"

Gently, he took her arm. "I'd like that. Stay at my place. I have plenty of room. Three bedrooms. You and Terry could each have your own and Owen can bunk with me."

"We'll be in touch." She handed him a slip of paper. "Terry's cell number and mine."

He nodded and slipped the paper into his pocket. He stooped in front of his son and handed him two business cards. "You take these, Owen. They have all my numbers and Pete Dugan's, too. In case you can't reach me, he'll know how to find me. Give the other to Terry, if she wants it. Will you do that for me?"

The child nodded, his expression grave. He was fighting back tears.

"Hey, buddy, we're gonna see each other very soon." He held out his arms and Owen flung himself into them.

'Why can't I stay here with you?" he said, sobbing now. "I want to stay here."

Demaris held him for a long time until Owen quieted. "Your mom would miss you too much."

"Won't you miss me?"

"I sure will, but I know we'll see each other soon. Take good care of Mom and Terry now, will you?"

He settled the boy in the car and closed the door, then came round to give Mary a hug and kiss. "Drive safe. See you soon."

"Thanks, Roger."

He nodded and stepped back, waving as they drove away. Only then did he allow the tears that had waited all day to fall. He had a son. Nothing else mattered at that moment besides his children. He had missed Terry terribly, and now there was Owen.

CHAPTER 38

"And, what do you have to say about your part in this mess, Mr. Stewart?"

For once, Stewart was not dressed in his trademark jogging clothes, but instead wore a white turtleneck, forest green cashmere sweater, and wrinkled corduroy slacks. The pants appeared to have had red wine splashed on them. He had been running fingers through his hair so that his comb-over now drooped to the left, exposing his bald pate. Demaris had never cared for turtlenecks on men, except on the ski slopes, where he seldom found himself.

"Go to hell. I'm tired and I want to call my attorney. He'll get me out of here and this hideous town as well. Where's June?"

"After your tantrum this evening, I would guess she's packing her bags for the earliest bus home."

"Yeah, right. Like she'd leave me."

Tired and eager to get back to the guest house with the team, he brought a stool into the cell and sat in front of Stewart, who slumped dejectedly on his cot, back to the cold cement wall. Pete stayed on the other side, seated in a metal folding chair next to the door.

"Okay, Mr. Stewart, we can make this brief, or we can be here all night. I understand that contrary to your previous statements you were suddenly professing deep, prior connections to the Winthrop family. How is it that you did not tell my detectives about this during your initial interview?"

"It was a long time ago. Our family summer homes were adjacent to each other in Maine. Bar Harbor."

"So I understand. So you knew the entire Winthrop family, then?"

"Vaguely. Our parents were friendly, cocktail party crowd. Harry Junior and his sister were younger than I was. We were in different crowds."

"Despite this vagueness and different crowds, you were nonetheless bragging to Mr. Hargreaves that you were a close family friend?"

"Hargreaves is an ass. I was sick of hearing how he and Harry were best friends. Which, according to my sources, was bullshit."

"And, who would those sources be?"

"Reynolds woman, mostly. She claims they were estranged."

"I see, well, we'll check into that. I wonder why you'd care what Mr. Hargreaves says and does. Did you know him prior to this weekend?"

"No, but he's an ingratiating know-it-all and I'm ready to go home."

Pot calling the kettle black, Demaris mused, rising and taking the stool with him. "Well, have a good night, Mr. Stewart. I'll see that you get your phone call now."

"What about my getting out of here?"

"That's up to the local police. The disturbance is their concern, not mine. There's also the damage to the Tavern. There'll be restitution costs. I'm sure your lawyer will sort things out. Goodnight."

He and Pete exited quickly, closing the door before Stewart could issue any further complaints. While they had been speaking to him, Hargreaves had been taken from his cell, adjacent to Stewart's, and placed in one of the station offices where Greta and Stevens were just completing their interview. When they appeared at the door, Greta started to rise and Demaris waved her down. "Stay as you are, Detective. I just have a couple of questions for Mr. Hargreaves."

"What? Stewart more important than me? I get the underlings and he gets the big chief?" He started to stand, but Stevens took hold of his shoulder.

Where was the man's affability now? And, what was with these people and their infinite capacity for snobbishness? Still dressed in faded blue jeans and sweatshirt, Hargreaves' pants also seemed to have sustained a splashing with red wine in the scuffle.

"Well, fortunately for you, the big chief is here now. Sit."

Hargreaves settled down, bringing elbows to knees, head resting on his hands.

"I assume you've given my detectives a rundown of your version of the row at the Tavern so I won't revisit that. I'm interested in whether there's any truth to the rumor that you and Harry Winthrop were estranged."

"None whatsoever. That's the most ridiculous thing I've ever heard. Who told you that?"

"Does it matter?"

"Look, we haven't seen much of each other since out last trip together, but I've been to Boston a couple of times. We always get together, as I told you."

"Was there an incident during your travels?"

"Minor one, if you must know, but we worked it out."

"Enlighten me."

"We were both interested in the same woman. I saw her first, Harry turned on the charm. Minor dust up when she jumped ship, but then she left town and that was that. We spent three months together after Madrid. That's where we sparred over the fair Sophie."

"What kind of sparring?"

"Verbal, maybe a couple of shoves. We were traveling. These things happen. Familiarity breeds contempt and all that. We moved on. No estrangement, end of story. Now can I get out of here, please?"

"As I told Mr. Stewart, that's up to the local police. Your mess happened in their town and has nothing to do with me. I believe Mr. Stewart is phoning his attorney."

"What a load of crap."

Demaris motioned to Stevens who disappeared and returned almost immediately with two of his fellow officers.

"Goodnight, Mr. Hargreaves. Oh, and stay away from Mr. Winthrop and Ms. Dore. They are planning a funeral for their loved one and they don't need you pestering them."

"I'm a family friend and you have no right to—"

"If you go near them, I will see that you are arrested for harassment. Do I make myself clear?"

"Just 'cause she's your old girlfriend doesn't give you the right to bar a family friend from offering support."

"Be very careful, Mr. Hargreaves." Breathing deeply, Demaris willed his voice to calmness. "Since you only met Ms. Dore two days ago and haven't seen Mr. Winthrop in many years, I hardly think they would characterize you as a family friend. They neither welcome nor want you solicitude. Thank you, officers. Take him away."

Pete watched his boss, who white knuckled the doorframe as Hargreaves passed by. "Ready to go back, boss?"

Lost in thought, Demaris took a minute before replying. "Yup, let's go."

They spent an hour debriefing. Stevens had spoken to Becca Rollins and Joan Nettleman, both of whom confirmed the time and duration of Burnham's visit to the dorm and Greta and Pete gave a recap of their interview with Hargreaves. Before the team broke for the night, he gave all three tasks for the following morning. He asked Stevens to get statements from the book club ladies and check Wolfson's claim about the Harbor Gym visit, which, in all the craziness of the day, they had neglected.

"Greta, I want you to find out what you can about this Sophie and the business in Madrid. Someone's got to know something. Maybe the Reynolds woman. She'll at least know where they stayed."

"Pete, find out what you can about the Bar Harbor days, although my gut tells me that's a dead end. Why the hell were Wolfson and Littlefield baiting the other two bozos? See what you can find out about that."

"What about you, boss?" Pete asked.

"I want to chat with Liz Reynolds again and poke around a little about the background of the new assistant headmaster. There's something he's not telling me and I want to know what. Maybe Jane Fellows would know. Is she back at her place now, does anyone know?"

"Now that Bess' mom's there, I think so," Pete said.

"Well, goodnight everyone. Get some rest."

Stevens went home and Pete to the guest house bedroom, while Demaris and Greta headed for their rooms at the B&B in Lois and Cathy's private quarters. Their private guest rooms were tiny, but each had a private bath and Lois had assured him the beds were comfortable. Wafts of cinnamon greeted them inside the front door and Lois appeared from the kitchen.

"Hey, you two. Want a fresh sticky bun? We're making them now for breakfast."

"Thanks, Lo. They smell incredible, but I had a huge meal and I'm beat."

"I'm in," Greta said. "Only had a bowl of soup for dinner."

Lois laughed. "Cathy's in the kitchen. Go through and she'll make you a cup of tea."

"Well, goodnight, sir."

"Goodnight, good work today."

When the kitchen door closed behind her, Lois turned to him. "Here's your key."

"Thanks."

Her old friend looked weary, but his eyes held a light she hadn't seen in a long time. "I hear you had a visitor today."

"Did you see him?"

"Yup, they came here looking for you first before they found Pete. I thought I was in the middle of that movie, *Honey I Shrunk the Lieutenant*. He's the image of you, isn't he?"

"Owen."

"Mary gonna bring him back?" Lois had never liked Mary and thought she had treated her friend very badly. Hands on hips, she gave him a stern look, somewhat softened by the flour that covered her nose and cheeks. Despite her tone, he couldn't help grinning at his champion standing before him, spatula in hand.

"Thanksgiving."

"It wasn't right of her."

"No, but it's done."

"She's a vindictive you-know-what, Roger."

"Maybe, but she deserved much better than me."

"That's bullshit. She played with you for years, while screwing around with anyone she could grab hold of."

"Now, now, I already have Pete clucking around. I don't need another Mother Hen."

"Yes, you do. You should go for joint custody. And, once the grieving period's over, isn't it time you made your feelings known to a certain local school teacher?"

"Okay, okay, now I know it's time for bed. Night, Lo. Thanks for squeezing us in. Better get out there if you want any buns for the breakfast crowd. Burke's a voracious eater and she loves pastry."

CHAPTER 39

"Roger, good morning! Come join us!" Mary Ann Morgan, one of the book club ladies and a local resident waved at him from a long table where she sat with the other seven members of the club and the librarian, Wilma Conlon, whom they appeared to have adopted. Greta was nowhere in sight.

"Good morning, ladies, that's very tempting, but I'm 'fraid I can't."

"Oh, why not?" Betty Sue, owner of the Bakery on Main, said, waving a sticky roll drenched in white frosting. "You've got to eat, Rodge."

"Perhaps, but not that."

"And, I hope you haven't been visiting Betty Sue and Frank's establishment since your heart attack." Mary Ann said. She a receptionist for Doctor Collins, the local G.P., but had yet to grasp the importance of confidentiality.

Cathy emerged from the kitchen carrying plates, three balanced on one arm, two on the other, followed by her partner. Lois had only three plates and a basket of muffins tucked in the crook of her arm. The plates, loaded with eggs, hash browns, bacon, and sausages, were soon set before the appreciative group and it was all he could do not to snitch a piece of crisp bacon from Mary Ann's plate.

"Sit anywhere," Lois said. "You want something?"

"No, thanks, Lo."

"I have oatmeal, gluten free, steel cut all prepared," Cathy said, grabbing a pitcher of fresh squeezed orange juice to refresh glasses.

Both proprietors were dressed in jeans, pale lilac, Honeysuckle B&B tee shirts, and aprons. Lois' was already smeared with something brown. Cathy's jeans hung on her lanky frame, while Lois' hugged every inch from her hips to her ankles.

"Oh, why not?" He smiled, turning to find a seat at one of the empty tables. "Maybe throw some walnuts in. I'd love some of that juice, too, and coffee?"

"Comin' right up," Cathy said, disappearing into the kitchen, Lois on her heels.

"Oh, no, you don't, Rodge. Come sit here," Betty Sue said, nudging her fellow diner, Suzanna, a part-time Bakery employee. They both scooted their chairs to the right and Mary Ann to the left, leaving just enough space for one more chair.

Suzanna and Vicky Brown were the youngest members of the book club. Both in their twenties, most of the others had at least twenty years on them. They lived together in a condo on the outskirts of Old Harbor. The Glen had about forty units tucked alongside the river that defined the village's western border. Demaris had considered buying a unit there when he sold his house, but bought in Bentley, a small community thirty minutes from Old Harbor, but only ten minutes from the regional office in Taunton.

Suzanna and Vicky were both teachers in Northport, the former, middle school science, the latter, first grade. Suzanna worked some afternoons and weekends at the Bakery. They were both slim, with long dark hair, Vicky's features delicate with alabaster skin, Suzanna, ruddier with freckles splayed over a turned-up nose. Demaris knew them both and had watched them grow up. Vicky's mom, Gretchen was Claire Rubin's close friend. Gretchen now lived in Florida, but secured invitations to join the book group for both her daughter and her friend. As soon as he was settled, juice and coffee in front of him, oatmeal on its way, Mary Ann turned to him. "Okay, Rodge, tell. We want to hear all the details. Don't leave a thing out."

He spied Esther McPhee across the table, an imperceptible shake of her head, before she turned her attention to her food. .

"Let the man be," Claire pronounced from her spot at the head of the table. "He's probably starved."

"I'm 'fraid I can't tell you much. Have you any thoughts you'd like to share?"

He was accustomed to seeing Mary Ann Morgan in her sedate, pink or pale green receptionist's uniform, which hugged every curve of her curvaceous figure. This morning she was dressed in bright yellow leggings and long, striped tunic, its colors reminiscent of a circus tent. Green eyes danced with mischief as she smoothed her shoulder-length auburn hair from her face. Despite the cooler weather, her feet were bare, her flip flops kicked off under the table.

"Yeah, right, like anyone tells us anything."

"I understand you all witnessed the scuffle between the two gentlemen last night?"

"Dreadful. So embarrassing to see two grown men behaving that way," Wilma Conlon said. "With those young people watching, too. What kind of an example do they set?"

"You mean the kitchen staff?"

"Yes," Mary Ann replied. "Everyone ran out of the kitchen to help break it up. Those two imbeciles with them certainly weren't helping."

"You mean Mr. Littlefield and Mr. Wolfson?"

Betty Sue leaned into the table, peering at him around her fellow diners. "Well, the bookseller was just plain smashed."

"Completely useless," Claire said. "And, ladies, we are never reading another mystery that is published by that horrid Mr. Littlefield."

"Good luck with that," Wilma said. "The Littlefield Group specializes in mysteries and they have 'em all."

"It's disgusting how these Internet companies have taken over, isn't it?" Lee Myers chimed in from the other end of the table.

Mary Ann leaned over and peered down the table. "Move with the times, Lee. Besides, you'd have never met your cutie biology professor if it hadn't been for the Internet."

Lee glared at her companion. "You don't know what you're talking about, M.A."

A handsome, fifty-something woman with short, wavy salt-and-pepper hair, and piercing blue eyes, Lee Myers was divorced for almost two decades after escaping an alcoholic husband who had abused her physically and emotionally. For many years, she had made an excellent living writing travel guides, but paper travel guides were rapidly disappearing, replaced by digital phone apps. Apparently, Lee had not moved with the times there, either. Pete had learned that Lee had occasionally encountered Tim and Harry in her travels. He made a mental note to ask her if she might have seen them in Madrid. Lee was also Claire's sister-in-law, from Claire's first marriage to her beloved brother Dicky. She had never warmed to Steele Rubin, but was cordial to him for Claire's sake.

Demaris' oatmeal arrived and he enjoyed it, listening to the ladies repartee. He was just about to excuse himself when Ben Silverman and Libby Drake appeared in the dining room. As Lois greeted them and ushered them to a table at the far end near the front bay window, Wilma Conlon leaned across the table and whispered, "You should talk to that pair, Lieutenant. They were there last night, but disappeared like a puff of smoke when the trouble began."

"She's right, "Mary Ann whispered. "He's a slimy one, too. A real narcissist."

Pete and Greta had interviewed the husband and wife. Their impression had not been favorable, as he recalled. Successful owners of a jewelry company in Providence, he was a world renowned tactician, sought after in his free time to sail on the yachts of the rich and famous. The success of the company as well as the raising of their two children had fallen mostly to her. The wife had pulled Greta aside to divulge that the Anne Greyson weekend had been her idea, one last desperate attempt to save a crumbling marriage torn asunder by his very public affairs, and her more discreet dalliances. She loved mysteries and Anne Greyson. He loathed them, but had read all of the author's books in preparation for the weekend and now considered himself an expert.

Libby Drake had also told Greta that on one of the infrequent times when she accompanied her husband sailing, they had entertained Tim Hargreaves and Harry Winthrop on a boat in Marbella. Greta's notes came back to him as Demaris watched Libby Drake order her breakfast. "We'd had a lot to drink. Harry Winthrop was a gorgeous, unattached man. For all I know, Ben could have hooked up with one of the staff that night. He was definitely screwing around with the cook on that trip, the pig."

He pushed back from the table, rising. "Well, ladies, this has been grand, but I've got to get cracking."

Mary Ann hopped up and pulled him aside. "Rodge, you know I've got my certificate as a marksman. Got it last summer. And, I've been an archer for years. If I can help, with the business of poor Harry's death, please let me know."

"Thanks, Mary Ann, I think we'll take you up on that offer. Are you attending the service?"

"Of course."

"Perhaps afterwards I could ask you and Mr. Hargreaves, who is also a competent archer, to speak with us?"

"Absolutely." Patting his arm, she winked, then turned back to her companions.

Demaris crossed the room and greeted the husband and wife. Both about his age, Silverman was handsome and he knew it. His dark wavy hair curled at his shoulders and his coal black bedroom eyes would make any woman swoon. He was dressed in khakis, boat shoes, and an open-collared blue shirt, a gray sweater draped over his slim shoulders. She was attractive, but he wondered if a former beauty might have been prematurely chipped away by painful married life. Slim, with crystal clear blue eyes, she wore her hair in wiry, bleach blond curls. She had a warm and genuine smile in sharp contrast to her husband's grimace. During their interviews, the team had uncovered an interesting connection between Libby Drake and Harry Winthrop. Pete and Greta had learned that Libby had attended Concord Academy at the same time as Honor Winthrop, Harry's sister.

"Hello, Lieutenant. Care to join us?" he asked.

"Thanks, but I'm on my way out. The ladies tell me that you were both present during the altercation with Mr. Hargreaves and Mr. Stewart last night. Is this correct?"

She looked stricken, but if the question unsettled him, her husband didn't show it. "Yes, we were there, why?" he replied, reaching for his coffee cup.

"Just curious if you noticed anything. I won't bother your breakfast, but I will send one or two of my detectives to talk with you later, if that's okay?"

"No, it is not okay. We're sick of this whole thing. Look, you can see how upset my wife is. This was supposed to be a relaxing weekend in the country for us and look at what it's turned into."

Libby Drake's eyes had filled up. "It's all right, Ben."

"No, it is not. There, see what you've done." He waved his hand in his wife's direction.

"Well, I'll let you get on with breakfast. I'm sorry the weekend has turned out poorly, but it turned out a damn sight more poorly for Harry Winthrop and Ralph Boardman. I'll see that my detectives are brief and to the point. Good morning." He smiled down at her, and turned away just as Lois served their plates, giving him a sly wink.

"Here we go, folks, egg white omelets and dry toast. Will there be anything else?"

CHAPTER 40

When he arrived at the guest house, the room smelled of coffee and sage. Greta, Pete, and Stevens were polishing off plates of eggs, sausage, and potatoes, an enormous basket of muffins in the center of the table.

Mouth full, Pete waved. "Have you eaten, boss? Tilly's taken good care of us and told me to phone your order over when you arrived."

He smiled at his assistant, who at that moment looked like a ten-year-old in a candy shop, tie loosened, hair rumpled. "So much for the non-competing agreement. I thought the Tavern stayed away from serving breakfast?"

"No charge. Tilly came in specially to make this for us," Stevens said as he grabbed an enormous blueberry muffin from the basket.

Greta laughed, her plate empty as she sipped coffee and watched her companions gorge themselves." It's really good, boss. Let Pete call over for you."

"Thanks, but I've eaten." He poured coffee and came to sit, filling them in on his breakfast at the B&B, as Greta took notes. "I want all you can dig up on Ben Silverman and Libby Drake. He's a prick, I don't trust him and I wanna know why the hell they ran out in the middle of Hargreaves and Stewart's lovers' quarrel. She's a sweetheart, but like about a zillion other women, she may have had a fling with Harry on their yacht a year or so ago."

Greta paused in her scribbling. "You know, boss. He was charmer and gorgeous, but I think Harry Winthrop's reputation as a ladies man may be overblown."

"Oh?" Demaris stared at his detective, her sharp hazel eyes shining with intelligence. By far the most observant detective with whom he had ever worked, she didn't miss much. Saddled with an invalid mother and no time for a social life, the job was her life. That aspect of Greta reminded him of himself and always made him wistful.

"I mean, the ladies loved him, don't get me wrong. They swooned over him on every continent from what we can gather, but Harry didn't often reciprocate beyond mild flirtation."

"Well, we've racked up an impressive list of these women from Libby Drake, the Reynolds woman, and the mysterious Sophie from Madrid."

"Oh, yes, sir, I have something on that," Stevens said, reluctantly setting his muffin aside and grabbing his notebook. "Sophie Calivera works for Santander, the bank. She's a senior VP and did, indeed, meet up with Mr. Winthrop and Mr. Hargreaves several years ago in Madrid, where she was on a business trip. Not sure who the winner was in that flirtation, but we've got a call in to Boston cops. They've agreed to catch up with her tomorrow."

"Good work, Stevens."

"But, that's not the most interesting part, sir."

"Oh?" Demaris gave the young officer a hard look.

Beaming, Stevens looked like the cat after it swallowed the canary. He sat up straighter, uniform pressed and clean, tie straight, every hair in place. "Yes, sir, there's more, sir. Guess who Ms. Calivera just recently broke up with?"

"Too early for guessing, son. Out with it."

"She and Boyle Wolfson have been dating for over a year. She dumped him last month."

"Anything else?"

"She's out of town right now, but due in tonight. Her roommate told me that she broke it off because of Wolfson's drinking, but she, the roommate, thinks Ms. Calivera's in love with someone else."

"Who?"

"She didn't know. Apparently, Ms. Calivera has been pretty secretive lately."

"Thanks, Brendan. Keep me posted. We've got a busy day ahead of us."

He turned to Greta and asked her to talk to Libby Drake and Ben Silverman about what they heard and saw at the Tavern. "And, if he gives you any crap, throw him in a cell."

"Pete, let's head over to the inn and roust the Reynolds woman. We also need a few minutes with Mary Ann Morgan and Hargreaves. Greta, try to get them over here around noon, if you would, and have one of Megan's crew bring down the arrow that killed Harry Winthrop?"

"Why, boss?" Pete asked, clearing plates and straightening his tie, pleased to be where he belonged, Demaris' side.

"They seem to be our archery experts and I'm curious what they make of that arrow. It's a bit unusual and Megan hasn't been able to learn much about it."

At that moment, his cell phone rang and he looked down, surprised to spy Bess' number. Immediately, he stood and excused himself, heading for the door. "Hey," he said, stepping outside and closing the door.

"It's her," Pete said, turning to Greta, shaking his head and rolling his eyes.

"Who?" Stevens asked, looking from one to the other of his companions.

"Jesus Christ, just when we're getting back to normal, she calls."

"Who?" Stevens asked again.

Greta eyed Dugan, placing a hand on his arm. "Leave it be, Pete."

"You heard him. He was finally talking like himself again, now who knows what he'll want to do."

"Hush," she said as the door opened.

"Look, you guys, I've got to be at the school for a short while."

"What for?" Pete asked.

"Ms. Dore has asked to speak to me."

"I'll go with you."

"Thanks, Pete, but I need you with the Reynolds woman. I want answers, clear answers, about her whereabouts for both murders. I also want a more truthful answer about what she knows about Harry's estrangement with Hargreaves. She knows much more than she's telling."

"We can do that after we go to the school and—"

Demaris took several deep, slow breaths before looking up at his assistant, knowing what he'd see in the pale, blue eyes—fear and concern. "No, we cannot.

You will find the Reynolds woman now and I will call after I speak with Ms. Dore. We can meet up at the Tavern or here. Is that clear?"

"But—"

Demaris' hand shot up, silencing Dugan, whose face was now red as a beet.

"Yes, sir, whatever you say, sir."

Pete slammed out of the room, leaving Stevens slack-jawed and Greta, head down, gathering her things. "Come on, Brendan, time to get cracking," she said, afraid to look in their boss' direction.

CHAPTER 41

As he drove through campus and parked behind the Meeting House, Demaris wondered, again, at the reason for Bess' call. Her voice was shaky, but not unexpected, given that the memorial for her beloved fiancé was this afternoon, only three days after his murder. The campus was blanketed in leaves, freshly fallen, and the maintenance crew had just begun their raking and leaf blowing. By the time people filed into the Meeting House at four, the grounds would be pristine.

The earthy, damp scent of fall leaves evoked memories of a fall long ago, when two lovers had walked hand in hand across this lovely campus, across its rolling lawns and into the woods beyond, where he spread his jacket and they lay, entwined in one another's arms. He could still smell the scent of orange and feel her softness against his chest, still hear her murmurs as they made love.

Lost in his reverie, he almost walked straight into Louie Predo, one of the gardeners. "Not quite right" in his mind and somewhat skittish, Louie knew him and therefore, stepped aside with a wave and "hi."

"Hello, Louie. It's been a while. How are you?"

"She's fine, she's fine. When is Billy coming back?"

Louie never made much sense, but Demaris knew who Billy was—Louie's former roommate and the man who had killed comptroller, Milt Wickie ten months earlier. He had still been with the Old Harbor Police Department back then. It had been his case. Discovering Billy Blackburn's guilt had given him no pleasure. The comptroller had been a nasty piece of work and Billy's suicide, a tragedy. They had never told Louie about Billy's death and he still looked for him every day.

With a wave, Demaris proceeded into the large stone and wood barn that housed the art studios, a cavernous, newly renovated space that always smelled of linseed oil and fresh sawn wood. He headed up to the second floor where Bess' studio and office were located, the sound of muffled voices all around him. Students worked in various spaces. A class was in progress in the ceramics studio, and faculty and students conversed in offices along the hall. As he headed down the hall, Joan Nettleman, the middle school art teacher, appeared, a voluminous white, paint splattered smock covering what appeared to be a chartreuse pants suit.

"Hello, hello, if it isn't our home grown super sleuth, what brings you here? You're not seeking me, I hope. I'm in the middle of class."

"No, is Bess around?"

"End of the hall, studio on the left last time I saw her. Any luck with the investigation?"

"Not so far. Any leads for me?"

"'Fraid not. Far as I know Mr. Squeaky Clean was well liked and who would want to hurt poor Ralph Boardman? Certainly no one I know."

"Thanks, Joan. I won't keep you."

When he reached the studio, he spied Bess talking with a student as they studied his self-portrait, which looked like it belonged in the trash bin. It sounded as if the artist thought so as well, but Ms. Dore was trying to encourage him to keep working on it. She spotted him and waved, patting the young painter on the shoulder.

"Hi, Roger. We can talk in my office. Busier in here than I'd expected."

"Bess, what are you doing here?" he asked as she closed the door. "Shouldn't you be home? I'm sure no one at school expected you to be in."

""I'm not teaching. School's given as much time as I need. I'll probably come back full time next week. I just needed to get out of the house. My mother is driving me crazy. Don't misunderstand. She's been a godsend and a huge help, but you remember what she's like."

"Yes," he said, smiling warmly as he sat in one of the two chairs in front of her cluttered desk. It had been a while since he had been in her office and he noticed the many photos of Macomber Dore, which had dominated the wall and desk space up until Harry Winthrop appeared on the scene, were missing. One small framed photo of her and Harry leaning against a tree was the only photo visible.

She sat in the other chair, eyes soft as she gazed at him. "Roger, thank you for coming. I know you're probably swamped."

"No trouble at all." His instinct was to reach across and take her hand, but he resisted, not wanting to spook her. "Is there something you wanted to tell me or did you just need a break?"

"I wanted to know if you'd discovered anything."

"Lots of things, but so far none add up to murder."

"Can I help?"

"How much did Harry tell you about his past? His travels, friends, things like that?"

"Not much. I sensed he didn't like to talk about the past, that it was troubling to him, so I didn't ask."

"You hadn't met Tim Hargreaves before Thursday?"

"No, and he's still calling and stopping by. Mother has been a stalwart gate keeper. What could he want?"

"I haven't a clue, but I'll have another word with him. Has anyone else tried to reach you?"

"A number of the workshop attendees have phoned, mostly to offer condolences and ask about refunds."

"Can I ask you to make a list of those, or ask your mom to do it, when you have a chance?"

"Of course."

"What do you know about your interim head?"

"Well, he's not Peter, or Pru, but he's holding down the fort. He and Pru are supposed to be great fundraisers, but they're just now gearing up for the next Capital Campaign so time will tell. Since Mr. Winthrop Senior settled in Old Harbor, fundraising has lost some of its urgency. You know he's given the school millions."

"I understand that Mr. Burnham asked you out early in his tenure?"

"Yes, but he's asked every woman on this campus out, without much success, hence his newest conquest, Lana. I told him I was with Harry and that was the end of it." She gave him a small smile, her eyes lighting up for an instant.

He nodded. "Bess, can I ask you something which might be unsettling?"

"Of course." She stared at him, eyes full of concern.

"What did Harry tell you about his fiancée, Stella Lang?"

"Not much. That was a very painful subject. You know about the accident, of course. That's really all he ever told me."

"I'm sorry about the way I handled that last year."

"It's okay. I understood that you were in the middle of a murder investigation."

"Did he ever describe the kind of person she was?"

"No, but I got the impression that she was very sophisticated and stylish. Harry didn't tell me that, but once, Jane looked her up on the Internet and we read a bit about her on the society pages."

"Did he say much about Hargreaves?"

"No, maybe once or twice in describing his travels he might have mentioned him. Tim helped him brainstorm plot and character ideas for the first Anne Greyson book."

"Had you met Ben Silverman or Libby Drake before?"

"No, but Harry knew them. They're sailors and he saw them somewhere, maybe in Spain a few years ago?"

"Impressions?"

"Not really, but I got the feeling that he wasn't that excited about being here."

"What about Carrion Littlefield or Boyle Wolfson?"

"Never."

"Had you ever heard of John Stewart before?"

"Not until he registered for the weekend. I'm pretty sure Harry didn't know him either or he would have said. He had business dealings with Carrion, of course, through his publishing house. He knew the book club ladies because they're all local or in the vicinity and this is a small community of towns. Then, there is Liz, his assistant."

"You'd met her before?"

"Once, but only for a minute when she stopped by the house to drop off some papers."

'Thoughts about her?"

"She had a huge crush on Harry, but who didn't? Everybody loved him. I loved him." Tears filled her eyes. "Oh, Roger, I let myself love him and now he's gone."

"I'm so sorry, Bess," he said, softly, reaching to take her hands in his.

He was prepared for her to pull away, stand, retreat, anything, but instead, her trembling body quieted and she sat very still, eyes lowered. Her warmth and the touch of her soft hands took his breath away, but he breathed slowly and quietly, simply allowing himself to experience the pleasure of her nearness.

Finally, ever so slowly and gently, she withdrew her hands and set them in her lap. "Can I ask you something?"

"Of course, anything," he replied, voice gruff.

"You seem different these days, from when you were investigating Milt Wickie's death."

"Yes."

"Calmer, not so angry. Almost like—" She paused, then looked into the deep, gray-blue eyes. "Almost like you were when we were alone together all those years ago. Even then you had an angry face you showed most of the world, but it's gone now, isn't it?"

He chuckled. "Mostly, but it's been known to sneak up once in a while."

"But how?"

"Lots of things. The heart attack, the job change, those were huge. The first woke me up and said 'pay attention, you idiot.' The second got me out of the hornet's nest in Old Harbor. Not a happy group, as you know. I'm my own boss, most of the time. I have a great team."

"You took Pete with you?"

Another chuckle. "Old Mother Hen, you mean. Pete's different. He's the son I never had until Owen."

"He adores you."

He smiled, leaning back in his chair. "Not sure if I'd use that word, but the feeling's mutual."

"What happened to the anger?"

"After kicking, screaming, and a huge wake up call, I made a conscious decision to let go, of everything. Took a great course from an MD at the fitness center in Taunton, about five miles from my house. Most of it dealt with stress reduction, but the classes that grabbed me most were the ones where we practiced mindfulness. I started meditating daily, took up yoga. Don't laugh! I'm a real beginner, but I've been to a couple of retreats. Changed my life."

"I'm glad for you, Roger. It's almost like I have my friend back after—"

"Two decades? I hope so."

She blushed crimson, the look in his eyes completely transparent for an instant. Flustered, she stood. "Now, I'll let you go. I shouldn't have pulled you away from your work."

"I'm glad you did. Can I take you home?"

She shook her head as they stood facing each other. "Oh, Roger, what am I going to do?" Without warning, she flung herself into his arms.

Startled, he drew her close. "Hey, Bess, you're strong. You'll get through this. " After several minutes, he stepped back to study her. "Okay?"

"Not really, but I'll pull it together."

"I'm sure you will. Can I give you a lift?"

"No, thanks. I'm sure Mother's sent out the National Guard, I've been gone so long."

She grabbed the threadbare brocade satchel she used as a purse.

"I'll get out of your hair, then." He brought his hand to her cheek for an instant. "Call me anytime. Okay?"

As he gazed at her, Demaris thought that Bess Dore had never looked lovelier. He stepped out, unsure if his legs would carry him to his car. Her nearness and warmth had shaken him. He would have to work very hard to pull himself together before he met up with Pete, who would be watching his every move.

CHAPTER 42

The two men met outside the Tavern. Pete gave him the eagle eye, but Demaris avoided eye contact and squelched any inquiries about his chat with Bess Dore by demanding to know what he had learned from Liz Reynolds.

"Before you get all pissy, I haven't talked to the Reynolds woman yet, but there's something I think you should hear from Charlie Boardman."

"Where is she?"

"She was having her hair done down the street. I told her to phone when she was finished. She just called and I asked her to meet me in the guest house."

"Let's go, then. Is Charlie tending bar?"

"All afternoon."

"We'll catch up with him later, then."

When they opened the door, she was helping herself to a bottle of water from the fridge. "Thanks for coming, Ms. Reynolds. Only keep you a short time."

"I should hope so."

She sat at the table so Pete grabbed the notes and folders and pushed them aside. "We just need to account for your whereabouts for when Mr. Boardman was killed, if you don't mind?"

"Well, I do mind and I can't imagine why I would want to stick a pitchfork into a complete stranger."

"Didn't you meet him the day you delivered papers to Mr. Winthrop at the hall?"

"No, I went in the front door, stayed less than ten minutes and exited the same way. How would I have encountered a gardener, or whatever he was?"

"Maybe he was working in the front yard?" Pete said.

"Well, he wasn't and I wouldn't know him from a three-headed alien, but to answer your question, after that god-awful dinner, I went down to the parlor and enjoyed a glass of sherry with the inn's proprietor, then took a short walk before turning in."

"How well did you know Stella Lang?"

She turned to Demaris, surprised by the change of topic and his abrupt tone. "Not well. Of course, I met her a few times. She came to some of the parties I planned for Harry."

"Did you form an impression of her?"

"Not good enough for him, but he seems, seemed, to be relatively indiscriminant in his choice of women. I mean, look at Miss Mousy School Marm."

"And what exactly was it about Ms. Lang that was not up to par, may I ask?"

"She was pretty, of course, in an anorexic, scrawny way. Very stylish, always overdressed. Clothes cost a fortune. Very snobby and dismissive of people she didn't deem worthy of her attention. At one of Harry's gatherings, a dinner party for a few friends, which I had organized, caterer, menu, bartender, everything, she took right over as hostess. I stepped back, of course, but then she proceeded to treat me like a servant for the rest of the evening. 'Liz, bring this,' 'Liz serve that.'

"It was insulting and rude. Harry told her several times that the caterers would serve and that I was a guest, but she ignored him, as always, and continued to play the Queen Bee. It was a turf thing, you see. There couldn't be any other woman calling the shots when she was around."

"Was Mr. Hargreaves at that dinner?"

"Not that I recall. It was for two of his college roommates. Tim and Harry went to boarding school together, but not college."

"Did Mr. Winthrop seem happy with Ms. Lang?"

"Now that you ask, no. I mean, she was beautiful and accomplished, but they didn't exactly seem head over heels in love. It was almost as if she had a hold over him."

"How so?"

"I couldn't say, but in truth, she didn't treat him much better than she did me. It made me sad."

"Were you there for the row with Stewart and Hargreaves?"

"For a while, but it was so ridiculous and boring that I left and went back to my room for a catnap. Imagine two grown men arguing about who knew the Winthrops better and who should go console the mousy fiancée? How absurd is that? Embarrassing, really."

"Well, thank you, Ms. Reynolds. We're heading to the Tavern for a late lunch, if you'd like to join us?"

"No, thanks. Tempting, but I'm getting a sandwich at the bakery. They are to die for."

The taproom was empty when they arrived and found Charlie Boardman wiping down the tables. He waved and said he'd get rid of his bucket and rags in the kitchen and be right back.

"Okay, Pete, what's he gonna tell me?"

"Well, I'd just gotten into it when you called, but guess who his dad used to work for before he came to old man Winthrop?"

"Out with it."

"The Langs. He lived in Wilcox, Maine, a small town right outside of Bar Harbor where the Langs had a summer home, or huge estate by the sound of it. Charlie's dad was one of five groundskeepers."

"In close proximity to the Winthrops, I'd guess. Do some checking and see if that's where Harry met the first fiancée, Stella Lang."

Pete was still scribbling notes when Charlie Boardman emerged from the kitchen and they waved him over to where they sat at the far corner of the still deserted taproom.

"Hey, Charlie," Demaris said, indicating the chair beside him. "How are you doing? Your dad's service all planned?"

"My aunt Jean has taken charge, which is one of the reasons I'm working today. Had to get out of the house." Dark circles rimmed his brown eyes. He was so like his dad minus the rough edges from years spent outside in the elements.

He wore jeans and a clean white shirt, a soiled apron protecting what Demaris guessed would be his bartender uniform for the evening.

"Are you staying on the estate?"

He nodded. "Mr. Winthrop has been terrific. Says I can stay on for as long as I need, but as soon as my aunt and cousins leave, I'm going to move out."

"Oh?"

"He needs the space for a new person."

"Knowing Mr. Winthrop's generosity, I'm sure his offer was sincere. Losing his son, he also no doubt likes the idea of having a younger person around the place."

"Yes, I'm sure, but it's not right. Besides, I can't stay there without Dad."

"I'm sorry, son. Have you found a place?"

He nodded. "I'm moving in with Sid and Wendy. They have an extra bedroom and have been asking me for months to move in, but I didn't want to leave Dad."

"That's good news, then."

He nodded. "Not to be rude, sir, but I guarantee that when the first customer shows up, Rachel will have my ass if I'm not behind the bar. She's back and, as I'm sure you know, not warm and fuzzy like Tilly. Did you want to talk to me about something?"

"Yes, Pete tells me that your dad used to work for the Lang family in Maine, before he came to the Winthrop estate?"

"Yes, he was one of the grounds crew. That place made the Winthrops' look like a postage stamp. They had close to a thousand acres, I think. I only went out there once. Workers were not encouraged to bring gawkers, such as family or friends, anywhere near the place. Totally different atmosphere than the Winthrops. Made my mom crazy. She wanted to see the inside of the palace, but there was never the opportunity. I mean, the Langs were only there for a brief time in the summer, but the housekeeper was a drill sergeant and no one got through the front door of the mansion without her approval. My dad only got as far as the back kitchen in all the years he worked there."

"How many was that?"

"Well, I'm twenty-four and he was working there at least two or three years before I was born so I'd guess about twenty? We moved here shortly after Mom got sick."

"How did he find out about the position at the Winthrop estate?"

"Through young Mr. Winthrop, actually. He met Dad when he visited with his fiancée, Ms. Lang, and they hit it off. Mr. Winthrop would sneak off in the late afternoon while everyone was dressing for dinner and have a beer with Dad in the maintenance shed."

"Did you know him then?"

"Never met him till we moved down here. Really nice guy. He was good to us. They both were. His father took care of all of Mom's medical expenses, which were astronomical."

Demaris nodded. "He's a kind man. What drew your parents to this area?"

"You may know that the Langs died less than six months after their daughter, Mr. Winthrop's fiancée. The estate had been donated to the state. I think Dad could have stayed on, but my Aunt Jean lives in Providence and he thought, well, they both thought, it would be easier to have family close by. My mom's diagnosis was pretty clear and they knew it would be a difficult few years."

"She was a brave and courageous woman," he said, remembering Julia Boardman around town, bald head wrapped in a bandana or covered with a colorful wool hat from September to June.

"Yes, she was. Anyway, my dad wrote to Harry Winthrop inquiring if there might be work on the father's estate and we moved within a month."

"Did you ever meet Stella Lang?"

"No, sir, I never met any of them. We lived one town over and they never came into town, Bar Harbor, I mean, and certainly not where we lived. Their employees did all the shopping. They had a huge sailboat and every so often me or my friends would see it cruising. They didn't use it much except when the kids were around and even then, not much."

"Kids?"

He smiled. "Sorry, I know, they were twice my age, but we always called 'em 'the kids.' It was kind of a local joke."

"Ms. Lang had siblings, then?"

At that moment, Rachel Hawes emerged from the kitchen, the Tavern's front door swung open, and three locals came into the taproom.

"Yes, a brother and sister. I think she was in the middle, but as I said, I never laid eyes on them except from a considerable distance and I wasn't carrying binoculars. I couldn't tell you what they looked like, except vague recollections of dark-haired adults dressed in black in the grainy newspaper reports of the parents' death." He stood up. "Uh, oh, the boss lady's here. Gotta go."

"Thanks, Charlie." Demaris stood and laid a hand on his shoulder. "We'll see you tomorrow, if not before."

The polar opposite of her partner in life and business, Rachel Hawes approached them and set a stack of menus on the adjacent table. "Well, well, well, if it isn't the conquering hero returned home?"

He hugged the petite blonde. She was dressed casually in wool slacks and matching V-neck sweater in a pale beige, a single strand of pearls at her neck. "Hello, Rach, nice to see you. You're looking very well."

She smoothed back her shoulder-length hair, an unnecessary gesture since a wide velvet headband currently held every strand in place. "Someone has to maintain standards with my ditzy partner in the kitchen. You're looking well yourself. The new command must suit you."

He smiled warmly. "It does, thanks."

"Pete, good to see you, too, sweetie. Can I have Charlie pour you guys something?"

"No, thanks, Rach. We've got to get going."

"See you later, then?"

"Most likely."

"We're catering the reception after the service. At the estate. Too much for Molly Pierce at her age."

"Okay then, see you later."

The men exited the rear door and headed for the guest house, where they found Greta Burke waiting with arrow that had killed Harry Winthrop encased in plastic.

CHAPTER 43

"So, Greta, before Stevens gets back with our so-called archery experts, tell me what's new?"

"Not much, sir. Jane Fellows didn't have much to say about the new interim head, except that he seems to be getting the lay of the land and not making waves while the permanent head, Pru Marsden, is away. He's apparently attempted to date every single woman on campus with the possible exception of the Nettleman woman."

Demaris smiled, taking a bite of a delicious turkey sandwich Tilly had sent over. "What about Libby Drake? Did you find her?"

"We tried, but she gave us the slip. We'll catch her after the service, don't worry."

"I'll try to button hole her, too. Has Stevens eaten?"

"Just started on his meatball grinder when we realized it was time to go pick up Morgan and Hargreaves," she said, indicating a plate on the counter.

"Okay, when they get here, let Brendan eat. Then I want you two all over the Langs, the family of Harry's first fiancée. I want photos, info about all three siblings—schools, friends, whatever. Stella Lang had a brother and a sister and I want to talk to them. Find out where they are, pronto, please. I'm also thinking we need background on Silverman and Drake, Hargreaves, Wolfson, Littlefield, the McPhees, and Stewart that goes much further back. For the hell of it, look into Arthur Burnham, too. He's hiding something and I want to know what. Why'd he get divorced? Where's his wife now? Anything you can find.

"Pete and I will handle the arrow experts and you two get started. Keep Stevens on it all day and into the night until he finds me something. You make a start, then meet us in front of the Meeting House by quarter to four. I want three sets of eyes there, but Brendan can stay put. Okay?"

Before Greta had time to ask for more specifics, the door opened and Stevens appeared with Mary Ann Morgan and Tim Hargreaves, the latter two were dressed casually, he in his usual jeans and Mary Ann in the tunic outfit she had worn at breakfast. Demaris decided he preferred Mary Ann Morgan in her pink receptionist's uniform. He suspected that the fluorescent yellow leggings and a wild striped top could prompt a seizure if she spun around too quickly.

Demaris pushed the remains of his lunch aside. "Can we get you something? Officer Stevens, once you finish your lunch, Detective Burke has some work for you."

"Thank you, I just ate," Mary Ann said, sitting on the loveseat.

"Me, too," Hargreaves said, plunking down beside her. "But, I wouldn't say no to a bottle of water."

Pete jumped up to fetch the water and Demaris pulled a chair opposite the two, coffee table between them. He placed the plastic-wrapped arrow in front of them. "Thank you both for coming. What can you tell me about this?"

"May I?" Hargreaves said, reaching forward to pick it up.

"Of course."

They both studied the package for several minutes, her head practically resting on his shoulder.

Finally, Hargreaves turned to her. "Custom-made, wouldn't you say?"

"Absolutely. Have you found the company that made it?"

Ignoring the question, Demaris said, "Why custom?"

"Pipe racks arrows have no heft and they're not tapered like this, see? This kind of arrow has exceptional accuracy. Little wind resistance so it would shoot true."

"He or she would have used a light bow, I'd expect," she said. "The size I'd use."

He nodded. "Yep, anything else and he'd have overshot, big time."

Demaris couldn't decide if either had the slightest idea what they were talking about or whether they just liked to hear themselves talk. He suspected it was the latter, but asked, "Have you ever seen an arrow like this before?"

They both shook their heads, but then Mary Ann said, "Now that I think of it, someone at the range had some custom-made. Not like this exactly, but similar. They were made by a local woodworker. I could get you the name, if you like?"

"That would be very helpful. Thank you. I expect you'll want to get back and get ready for the service?"

CHAPTER 44

After making a phone call to Megan Kreiger, asking her to stand by at the lab, Demaris changed and met Pete at the car. He wasn't sure why he had asked Meg to come down, a hunch maybe, but she had gone home and she lived two hours away.

His assistant looked handsome in a dark blue suit, blue dress shirt, and subdued tie in green-and-navy stripes. He'd worn service dress shoes, polished so they shone like new. Demaris smiled, patting him on the shoulder before circling the car. "You drive."

They spied Greta beside the door, where Demaris had asked her to be at three thirty. He almost didn't recognize her in a gray-fitted suit, wide-brimmed hat, and heels. They were low, sensible heels, but they flattered her slim legs. Her hair, tamed by the hat, looked almost stylish and she wore a brightly colored scarf in blues, greens, and grays at her neck.

"You look lovely, Burke."

She blushed. "Thank you, sir. You guys don't look too shabby either."

"Find anything?"

"Not much. Stevens is hard at work. We've found plenty on Hargreaves and all his youthful run-ins with the law, but we're having trouble going back very far on the others. It's almost like John Stewart didn't exist until he started working for that investment company in Concord. Wolfson's past is fuzzy and Littlefield has all kinds of firewalls on his personal information, which isn't all that unusual in his line of work. Silverman spends a lot of time out of the country and his whereabouts and behavior are somewhat erratic."

"Pete, why don't you head in."

Pete nodded and disappeared without protest just as a group of mourners approached. Liz Reynolds nodded to them and walked by with Tim Hargreaves, dressed in a tweed sport coat and gray flannels. Demaris wondered if the death grip she had on Hargreaves' arm was amorous or for safety so she didn't topple over in her stiletto heels. Dressed in a black sheath and matching coat, her blond hair was swept up, the only color other than a floral infinity scarf around her slender throat.

Arthur Burnham passed by with Todd and Sheila Bridgham. The men wore charcoal gray suits, Sheila wore a black pencil skirt and a matching bolero jacket over a cream-colored blouse. They were followed by the Thurberts and a number of school people, including Jane Fellows, who winked at Demaris as she passed by. "A lot of the workshop people are already inside," Greta said, stepping closer, her voice a whisper. Stewart and Littlefield arrived together, no sign of Stewart's lady friend. Too bad, too, 'cause she might have been impressed by his four-thousand-dollar suit."

"You're kidding."

"Nope, Littlefield's, too. They were most likely custom-made by the cut of them."

"And, you know this because?"

"A few months back, I was bored so I studied high-end fashion mags, in case we ever needed to know."

"Really?" He looked at his detective, uncertain of whether she was teasing him.

"Well, sort of." She smiled at him. "Let's just say I keep up. And, my uncle is a tailor. Works with high-end clients. I helped out in the shop after school."

"What about Wolfson and the group that just passed?"

"Wolfson was in his usual tacky stuff. Navy sport coat and khakis. I mean, who wears that to a funeral? Both headmasters had nice suits, but strictly off the rack. Carrie Thurbert trying hard, but not that impressive although her dress might be an older Armani. Hargreaves is still going for the Mr. Chips rumpled look, nothing pricey there and his hanger on is in Ralph Lauren, nothing too pricey except her Jimmy Choos, which she could have gotten on sale. I mean, stilettos are so last year."

Demaris laughed. "And what does the fashion police woman make of my attire?"

"Surprised me, actually," she said, stepping back to survey his charcoal gray suit. "I figured you for something off the racks, maybe J.C. Penney, but that's a nice suit. Maybe fifteen hundred, two thousand? Brooks Brothers? Could be from the outlet, but it's been tailored for you. With your height and broad shoulders, I imagine it's hard to find something off the rack that fits."

"Pretty close. This is my wedding, funeral, and meet with the big brass suit. Last winter, shortly after I changed jobs, I was on State Street in Boston and I splurged."

"It hangs really well on you," she said, as they turned to see Mr. Winthrop and his staff as well as Bess and her mother making their way toward them. Molly Pierce held one of the old man's elbows, Helen Stevens the other. Bess and Maggie Guilford walked just behind them."

Lovely as always in a pale gray suit, Bess wore a soft wool scarf at her neck, and black low-heeled pumps. Hatless, strands of light brown hair blew across her face in the breeze and she brushed them away. As they passed by, she gave him a shy smile and nodded to his companion. With the exception of Mr. Winthrop, who gave a slight wave, the others did not seem to notice their presence.

"The mother's in Dior, this season," Greta whispered, regretting her words when she caught her boss' expression. The naked longing in his eyes as he watched Bess Dore took her breath away.

They were just about to enter when Ben Silverman and Libby Drake hurried up the walkway. Greta kept comments on their attire to herself, though she couldn't help but notice that he wore a tailored suit that rivaled Stewart's and his wife appeared to be in Stella McCarthy.

When everyone was seated, Demaris and Greta entered and stood just inside the door. They spied Pete seated on one of the side benches at the far end of the room and nodded. Shortly after, Jean Davol, a Board member and current Clerk of the Meeting, rose from her seat at the heart of the circled benches and welcomed everyone. She then read a short prayer by Rumi, which she stated had been selected by Harry Winthrop's father.

"This is a time for all to remember the life of Harold Chase Winthrop the second. We are gathered, his friends, family, and all who knew and loved him to celebrate a life well-lived. Let your heart be your guide. If you feel moved to speak, please do, leaving space between speakers for silence. Welcome and God bless."

Jean sat and silence enveloped the room. Many eyes turned to Bess, but Demaris guessed she would not speak. Tears already snaked down her cheeks. Her mother's arm circled her trembling shoulders.

After five minutes, Peter Thurbert rose. "Harry Winthrop was a wonderful, kind, and generous man. A blithe spirit, brought to our community by tragedy, he pitched in with our dedicated police force to help our school and village to heal and go on. He will be remembered by his many good works in Old Harbor, most undertaken quietly and anonymously. We all mourn his untimely passing and hope that through remembering we can and will keep him with us."

Thurbert had barely sat down when John Stewart popped up. "As a family friend of the Winthrops, I wanted to say how much my family admired Harry Winthrop and his many accomplishments."

Demaris had a clean line of vision to Harry Winthrop Senior who glared at Stewart, shaking his head. For an instant, he feared he might rise on trembling limbs to denounce the fatuous Stewart, but instead, he stared at the ground as Stewart droned on about summers in Maine and neighborhood barbecues. Finally, and mercifully, he sat down.

Not to be outdone, Tim Hargreaves stood several minutes later, wresting himself from Liz Reynolds' claw-like grasp to regale the assemblage with tales of his travels with Harry. "Harry and I go way back to Exeter days, he was the smart one and I was the jock. He was an amazing role model, a thinker, and a gifted writer, Anne Greyson notwithstanding. I've tried to live up to his example through my teaching and scholarship. His example will inspire me for the rest of my life."

After Hargreaves sat, there was a blissful ten minutes of silence before Wolfson stood to talk about the Anne Greyson books and the whimsy and joy they brought to loyal readers. "Anne Greyson and I kind of 'came out' together so to speak as her, or his, first book debuted shortly after I bought the shop from its longtime owner, whom, I suspect, would have loved the books as much as Harry's readers do. Unfortunately, he passed away shortly after retirement." When Wolfson sat, Claire Rubin, disregarding Jean Davol's request for silence, hopped up to speak briefly about the book group and their love of the Anne Greyson books. "Let me also say, that those of us who knew Mr. Winthrop, loved and respected him. In just a short time, he had become a pillar of our community. He volunteered at the boys and girls after school clubs, tutored at the libraries in both Old Harbor and Northport, and he never missed the opportunity to lend a hand at events like beach cleanup, Veterans suppers, and support for our senior citizens. I don't know how our communities will do without him."

Liz Reynolds waited about five minutes after Claire Rubin, then stood shakily on her high heels, pulling a slip of paper from her pocket. She cleared her throat, then began. "I have known dear Harry for many years and can honestly say that he was the best guy I've ever known, in every way. He was the kindest and most generous of bosses and my dearest friend. I…I…" Tears filled her eyes and after a few more attempts to keep talking, Tim Hargreaves persuaded her to sit, where she collapsed, sobbing against his shoulder.

Demaris attended Meeting for Worship on and off, and had for many years, but he found memorial services, which usually turned into "popcorn meetings" to be difficult to sit through. He was considering stepping out, when Helen Stevens stood.

"On behalf of the Winthrop household, may I say that Mr. Harry will be greatly missed for his kindness, warmth, generosity, and genuine respect for others. We were all so pleased about his upcoming nuptials. He was a different man this past year with Ms. Dore. She brought such joy back into his life, into all our lives, because we saw and knew that he was happy. Our deepest condolences to his beloved fiancée and, of course, to his dear father, whom we all love so much."

Not an eye was dry as the housekeeper sat, including her own. Molly Pierce reached over and took her trembling hand. Silence ensued for ten minutes and Demaris waited for the Clerk to stand and close the meeting when a tall, lanky stranger stood from the back row across the room.

"Hello, everyone. My name's Bill Jacobson. I was Harry's college roommate and a dear friend of many years. While we have seen little of each other in recent years, we have kept in touch by phone, e-mail, and the occasional lunch when I get to Cambridge. We've been through a lot together, joys, triumphs, and sorrows, Harry and I, and I cannot conceive of a world without him in it. In addition to all of his fine qualities others have mentioned, I wanted to mention his integrity. I have never met anyone I trusted more and whom I was always absolutely certain that whatever he said or did was both honorable and true.

"The last time I saw him was June, when we had lunch at the Harvard Club. He was a changed man. After the sorrow and blackness of years marked with tragedy after tragedy, he had found peace and happiness in this lovely village, with a woman he deeply loved. Over the years, I've seen my friend think he was 'in love' a few times, but nothing like I saw in June. He had found the love of his life and if he could have, he would have shouted his joy from the rooftops. My deepest condolences to his beloved father, Harry Winthrop Senior, and to you, Ms. Dore, for this terrible, terrible loss."

Jean Davol let Bill Jacobson's words resonate for almost twenty minutes in a silence both profound and reverent. Finally, she rose and closed the meeting with the poem "Crossing the Bar," which had apparently been one of Harry's favorites.

CHAPTER 45

As mourners filed from the white clapboard Meeting House, Demaris noticed Libby Drake, who emerged sobbing and inconsolable on her husband's arm. He was trying his best to ignore her and pretend all was well.

He approached the couple, eyes kind and solicitous. "Ms. Drake, I wonder if I might have a brief word?"

"Jesus Christ, man, can't you see that my wife is very distraught?"

"Yes, and I wouldn't intrude, if time was not of the essence. I would like to send you home, along with all the others, as soon as possible."

Silverman's eyes flashed fire. "We're leaving tonight."

"I'm not sure that will be possible."

"We're only in frigging Providence, for Christ's sake."

"It's all right, Ben," she said, extracting her elbow from his grasp. "Why don't you run down and get the car? Lieutenant Demaris and I will walk down and meet you. Go on, please."

"Fine, spill your guts. Go right ahead, what do I care? This weekend was the biggest mistake of my life." With that, her husband stomped off down the driveway to join the stream of mourners.

As Libby Drake turned to face him, a tremor coursed through her body.

"Are you cold? We can step inside if you like?"

"No, this is fine. The cold clears my head. Stuffy in the Meeting House, wasn't it?"

He nodded, kind eyes regarding her. He motioned to Greta to follow them and she pulled out her notebook and trailed a short distance behind.

"I gather the Anne Greyson weekend was your idea?"

"I dragged Ben to this. The service and the weekend. It was a last ditch effort to save a crumbling marriage."

"I'm sorry. Did Harry Winthrop have anything to do with your marital problems?"

"Absolutely not, why?"

"Well, Detective Burke mentioned your rendezvous with him and Mr. Hargreaves when you were abroad?"

"Yes, we entertained them when the boat was docked in Spain, in Marbella. It was a wild night. Lots of drinking, but nothing happened, at least not between me and Harry Winthrop."

"But, Detective Burke indicated that you might have had too much to drink and perhaps something occurred?"

"I'm sorry I misled her. If anything happened that night, it happened between me and Tim Hargreaves. Spite sex. I'd just joined Ben on the cruise the day before and it was obvious that he and the cook were screwing around. The sailing community is a tight-knit group. Not much stays secret and it's common knowledge that my husband sleeps with any woman who'll have him, on land or at sea. When I arrived and saw them together, I was furious that I'd bothered to arrange sitters for my kids only to come all that way and be slapped in the face with his adultery again.

"I flirted with Harry, yes, to make Ben jealous, but as his friend just told us, Mr. Winthrop had integrity, his friend did not. Harry was the only sober one among us. When he saw what was happening, he excused himself and, I assume, went back to his hotel. That would be after my dear husband had disappeared into the galley, no doubt to screw that skinny whore in the back pantry. Tim and I left the boat and headed into town. There's a nice little boutique hotel five blocks from the dock. I didn't say anything the other day because Ben sees Tim sometimes. They've been friends for years. Tim used to sail, but doesn't do much anymore."

"I see. So did your husband assume when you didn't come home that you'd spent the night with Harry Winthrop?"

"He didn't ask, doesn't care, and I saw no reason to keep him up to date on my liaisons."

"I see."

"I can see by your eyes that you're wondering why I'd want to save a marriage this horrible."

"We don't judge, Ms. Drake, but were you to ask me, I'd say you deserve better."

"It's the loss of my whole way of life, you see. Our entire social life revolves around sailing. If I walk away, their loyalty will be with Ben. I'll have no one."

Sounds like you've had no one for a long while, Demaris thought, watching her sadly. "Perhaps a new circle might present itself if you stepped away?"

"Perhaps. Is that all? As you can see, Ben is waving frantically over there."

She pointed to a beige Land Rover, which Silverman had pulled up on the grass not far from them.

"Greta, would you tell Mr. Silverman that we'll only be a minute, please?"

As his detective headed for the Land Rover, he turned to Libby. "Sorry for the grilling. You've been most helpful. I have one other question. Detective Burke tells me that you attended school with Honor Winthrop, Harry's sister."

"Yes, but I didn't know her well. She was three years younger than me. We were only there for one year at the same time. As you are no doubt aware, both Tim Hargreaves and Harry Winthrop are younger than Ben and me. Honor was, too."

"Impressions?"

"Sorry, I have none. She played field hockey and so did I, but I was on varsity and she only played with us once. She was beautiful, just like her brother. Her death, and that of her mother, were reported in our alumni magazine. Huge spread, because the family had been very generous to Concord. It was the late Mrs. Winthrop's alma mater."

"Thank you, Ms. Drake. Will you and your husband be coming to the reception at the estate?"

"I'd like to come, to pay my respects, but we'll see. Are we free to return to Providence?"

"Yes, but we'll be asking your husband to surrender his passport and to stay put until we complete our investigation."

She clapped her hand over her mouth and for an instant, he thought he heard a chuckle. "Oh, that'll go over real well."

"If I don't see you again, take care, Ms. Drake. And, good luck."

"I have two amazing kids. He did give me that." With a sad nod, she turned away."

CHAPTER 46

"Just look at him," Wolfson said, gesturing across the huge living room at Carrion Littlefield, who was chatting with Bess and her mother. "He calls himself a publisher, yet doesn't have a shred of regret about putting independent bookshops out of business."

The cavernous room boasted seven foot fireplaces at the north and south ends, a fire blazing in each. Priceless paintings and tapestry festooned three walls, the fourth, mostly floor-to-ceiling leaded glass, looked westward, the orangey gold of the sunset reflected on the assemblage. Originally designed as a ballroom, the space now had six sitting areas where guests could relax and enjoy drinks and food. The long tables that bisected the room's middle held platters of appetizers, whole hams, turkeys, and bowls filled with salads, breads, and fruit. Wait staff passed hot appetizers and three round tables scattered at various spots held mountains of cheese, desserts, and vegetables.

"E-books are here to stay, Wolfson. Better get over it," John Stewart said, rolling his eyes at Tim Hargreaves and Liz Reynolds, who stood beside him.

"He knows books," she said. "Wonder what he and the dumpy fiancée are so cozy about."

"What's your beef with the Dore woman?" Stewart asked. "You've been cutting her to pieces all weekend."

"Isn't it obvious?" Wolfson said, already appearing to be tipsy. "Our Liz was in love with Harry. Sees our schoolmarm as a rival."

"Don't be ridiculous. I couldn't care less about that mousy little creature."

"Who captured darling Harry's heart," Boyle said, tipping his glass to no one in particular.

"Cut it out, Boyle. This is neither the time nor the place," Hargreaves said, as he draped a protective arm over her shoulders.

"Boyle, you disgust me," she said, turning to walk away, practically colliding with Demaris and Dugan. It was clear they had heard the entire conversation.

"Lurking in the shadows, I see. When can I get out of here, Lieutenant?"

"We'll update you tomorrow."

As Reynolds stalked off toward the bar, Demaris watched Littlefield turn on the charm, addressing most of his remarks to Maggie Guilford, whom he appeared to have eating out of his hand.

"He's nice-looking. Gotta give him that," Jane Fellows whispered, coming to stand beside him. She looked particularly lovely in a green velvet jacket and flowing peasant skirt, a cream scarf at her neck, long auburn hair swept back in a loose braid.

He smiled at her. Jane was one of the few school people he genuinely liked. "I don't have to give him anything, but yes, he's good-looking. Successful, too, I understand."

'You don't 'spose he's trying to chat Bess up, do you?"

"Better not be." It slipped out before he could stop himself.

"Don't worry, she's immune to his type of charm. But, while we're on the subject, how long are you going to wait? Neither of you are getting any younger."

Demaris was grateful Pete had stepped away to intercept Greta at the side door and had not heard Jane's last remark. A flippant response on the tip of his tongue, he paused, then smiled. "We had our chance. Ancient history, I'm 'fraid."

"And here I thought you were some kind of brilliant detective."

She patted his arm and strolled off as Greta and Pete approached.

"Stevens has been a busy little beaver," she said, taking him aside. She still wore her suit, but it was now rumpled and several stains spotted the jacket. They appeared to be chili, most likely prepared and delivered to the guest house by Tilly. "He cannot find a trace of Stella Lang's brother, Julian, but he's found

Charlotte Lang and she'll see us tonight at seven. She lives in Providence. We've got the address."

"Good work. You go back and keep digging. Pete and I'll stay here till most people clear out."

With a "yes sir," Greta slipped out.

CHAPTER 47

The conversation between Maggie Guilford, her daughter, and Carrion Littlefield had begun with condolences, but almost immediately turned to his favorite subject, e-book publishing, and he was regaling the women with stories of overnight indie authors' successes as well as those traditionally published.

"You don't see Harry's editor and publisher from Mount Hope here, do you? The big houses, and even the mid-sizes houses like Mount Hope, couldn't be bothered promoting mid-list authors."

Rather in awe of the dashing publisher, Bess still felt compelled to defend Mount Hope, the house that had given Harry his start and had been so loyal in publishing and promoting his fiction and nonfiction books. "Robert Hale, Harry's editor, was signed up for the weekend, but he had a family crisis, and sent his regrets."

As she spoke, she noticed Roger from across the room and smiled. In truth, she had noticed him since the moment he walked in, first with Pete Dugan, then joined by Greta Burke. His presence made her feel safe and she found herself wishing he would come and stand beside her, instead of her mother, who was flirting shamelessly with Littlefield. She wondered if her thrice-married mother would ever realize that she would be seventy in three years and should not be flirting with men fifteen or twenty years younger, at least not with her daughter present.

Littlefield was older than her forty-two years, but not by much, she guessed. He was handsome and he knew it, but even with his expensive suits and flamboyant manner, there was something fragile about the man, something that made him very approachable.

Maggie Guilford waved her hand. "Oh, never mind about that, ancient history. What's done is done and poor Harry, whom I never met is gone." She dabbed at her dry eyes with a cocktail napkin. "I've always wanted to write a book, a memoir. I've led such a full, colorful life and I'm sure other women would be interested in my story."

Littlefield gave her a benevolent smile, setting his wine glass on a passing tray and motioning for another. "We usually try to publish books that appeal to both men and women. Wider market share that way."

"Oh, darling, my story will interest men, too. I did say colorful, didn't I?"

"Mother, would you like to sit down?"

"Oh, pish tush, of course not. Wish I had thought to ask for a refill."

"Well, I could get you one," he said, before glancing at Bess who was shaking her head "no."

"Ignore my daughter. I'll go ask that adorable bartender for another. Excuse me."

"Sorry, she has never been able to hold her liquor."

"She's delightful. You're lucky to have a parent so close by."

"Oh, but she's not! I would have killed her long ago. No, no, she and her third husband, Tim, live in Florida. She was coming up for the Anne Greyson weekend with the added bonus of meeting Harry before the wedding. Now she says she's staying on to take care of me. I'm trying to persuade her to go home tomorrow, but she insists she's staying all week, maybe longer."

"So, she liked Anne Greyson, too?"

"Yes, one of the few interests we have in common. I have to admit that Mother gave me the first in the series for Christmas a number of years ago, and I was hooked. I even went down last year to attend her book club's discussion of Book Three."

"Ah, I think that's my favorite."

"Mine, too, although I love them all."

"Then, why not continue them? Take over the writing yourself?"

Before she could answer, Wilma Conlon spoke from behind them, where she had obviously been eavesdropping. "Excellent idea!"

Startled, both of them turned to stare at the diminutive librarian, who stepped forward to join them, full glass of sherry in one hand, plate of appetizers in the other. "Sorry to break in, but I was coming to speak to Bess and couldn't help overhearing. I think continuing the series is a wonderful idea. What a fitting tribute to Mr. Winthrop. I'm sure he'd be pleased."

"Have you two lost your minds?" Bess stared from one to the other just as her mother returned with a huge glass of chardonnay. She would have to have a word with Charlie Boardman, who was tending bar.

Littlefield chuckled, clearly pleased at the reaction to his suggestion. "No, we haven't lost our minds. People do it all the time. Think *Nancy Drew, The Hardy Boys* and *Gone with the Wind.* Robert Parker's books have continued after his death, haven't they?"

"Well, I'm not Margaret Mitchell, Carolyn Keene or Robert Parker's ghost writer! I teach art and am a terrible writer."

"Nonsense, you were an excellent English student, my pet. She wrote wonderful essays and poems in high school and college. Then, what does she do, but follow her husband's dream and become an art teacher in a little village in the middle of nowhere."

"Mother, that's enough. You haven't the faintest idea what you're talking about."

Littlefield could sense the conversation derailing and moved to Maggie Guilford's side. "Let's not get testy. Our lovely local librarian, Wendy, and I were simply playing around with the idea of continuing the Greyson series. Playing, nothing serious."

"It's Wilma," Conlon said, but no one heard.

Basking in the light of his flirtatious attentions, Maggie Guilford forgot all about her daughter and her career choices. "I love play, Carrie darling."

"Okay, that's enough. Mother, I want you to sit down and eat something, now. Excuse us, would you?"

Observing her friend's distress, Jane Fellows crossed the room and took Maggie's arm, guiding her to a leather couch in an area of the room where the book club members had congregated. "Maggie, we've barely had a minute to catch up. Come sit and tell me about life in Vero and that handsome hubby of yours, Tim, isn't it? Bess tells me that after nearly five years, he finally made an honest woman out of you."

Bess mouthed, "thank you" to her friend, listening as Maggie launched into a description of her impromptu, but elegant nuptials. Stepping back, she breathed a sigh of relief for the unexpected respite and turned, intending to go and keep Mr. Winthrop company for a while, when her former companions intercepted her.

"Think about it, Bess," Littlefield said.

"I have thought about it and the answer is no. It's ridiculous."

"No, it's not. You could do it, and I could help," Wilma said. "I love to proofread things and do it all the time for library patrons."

"It's not the proofing, Wilma, it's the rest of it. I am not a mystery writer! I love to read mysteries, but wouldn't have the faintest idea of how to write one. Now, if you'll both excuse me, I'd like to sit with Harry's dad for a while."

Littlefield tipped his wine in toast. "I'll give you a month or two, then be in contact. My group could publish the next book as a first run indie and we'd see how they went. Or, you can try and get Mount Hope on board. What do you say, we talk after the holidays?"

"Won't matter in the slightest. I am not changing my mind!" she sputtered, turning so fast that she ran right into him. He reached out and caught her shoulders, preventing a headlong fall into the cheese table.

"Roger, oh, I'm sorry! Thank goodness I wasn't carrying a drink."

"You okay? Was Littlefield pestering you?"

"No, he's actually not a bad sort. He's been very kind since—" Tears sprung up and she shook her head. "It's my mother, being her usual inappropriate self. Then Carrion made a suggestion that Wilma Conlon hopped right on and suddenly the conversation turned to the absurd. I'm not in the mood for absurd, or my mother today. I thought I should go and sit with Mr. Winthrop for a while. He looks sad and lonely in that big chair."

He let go of her shoulders. "Okay, I'll come with you. What kind of suggestion?"

"They want me to continue writing the Anne Greyson books. Isn't that the most ridiculous thing you've ever heard?"

Actually, no, he thought, but stayed silent, not wanting to upset her further. As they reached Harry Winthrop Senior's circle, which included Molly Pierce and Helen Stevens, perched in stiff wooden chairs on either side of their employer, Pete interrupted. He waited as Molly rose and ceded her chair to Bess before turning to his assistant.

"Yes?"

"Ben Silverman and his wife just walked in and he wants to speak to you, pronto."

"Did you ask him what he wants?"

"Yes, and he says he doesn't talk to underlings."

"I'll be over in a minute. Why don't you try to be gallant and get Libby Drake a drink? I'm sure her husband won't think of it."

CHAPTER 48

"How are you, Mr. Winthrop?" Demaris said, taking the chair on the other side of their host vacated by Helen Stevens. Both Molly Pierce and Helen retreated into the shadows, apparently reassured that their beloved employer was safe with Bess and Roger.

Watery, bloodshot eyes regarded him, an infinite well of sadness in their depths. "I'll be better when you find the monster, Lieutenant. Once that happens, I'm planning to close my eyes and join my wife and children."

"We will, sir." Demaris leaned closer so that only his host could hear him. "Are you up to one question?" Winthrop nodded. "What can you tell me about the McPhees and your business deal gone south? Any chance he'd retaliate?"

"Lionel McPhee's an ass, but he couldn't hurt a fly. Worst businessman I've ever known. Always had a grandiose, get-rich-quick scheme. Most never got off the ground. No one would invest in his fly-by-night ideas."

"According to his wife, he lost all his money on that land deal with you."

"Don't you believe it. Esther's a bubblehead and a gold digger. She doesn't know the first thing about Lionel's finances, I guarantee it. Oh, he lived rich, but there was never much there."

"Did your pulling out sour the land deal?"

"Nope. The state scotched that scheme, but by then Lionel was so far in the hole he wasn't ever gonna see daylight."

"Did he blame you?"

"Better not. How do you think he's still living in Mattapoisett? Not on the income from the piddly little shop of Esther's."

"You mean you helped financially?"

"Let's just say I had my attorneys mop up his mess and set up a small income for old Li."

"Why would you do that?"

"His first wife and my dear Catherine were good friends. Let's call it a memorial to my beloved Cathy. She would have wanted me to help."

Tears snaked down the wizened cheeks and Winthrop slumped forward. They each grabbed an elbow and supported him as Molly appeared from behind.

Bess placed a napkin in his lap, which he used to wipe away the tears. "You're tired, Mr. Winthrop. Can we help you to somewhere to lie down?"

Winthrop straightened and leaned back in his chair. "No, dear Bess. I want to see this through. Hopefully this crowd will thin out soon."

"We can help with that. Just say the word and they're gone," Demaris said, standing up. "Now, if you'll excuse me?"

"I'm counting on you, Lieutenant." Winthrop called as Molly took the chair beside him and Bess ceded hers to Helen Stevens.

Reluctantly, he approached Ben Silverman, who stood beside his wife at the edge of the crowd, stony and silent. Demaris noticed that she held a glass of wine; he did not. "I heard you wanted to speak with me?"

Libby Drake took a step forward away from her husband. "Ah, Lieutenant, now that you're here, I'll excuse myself and pay my respects to Mr. Winthrop."

Demaris smiled and nodded as she practically ran by him. "Of course." He turned to Ben Silverman, eyes questioning. "How can I help you?"

"Well, first, you can tell me what the hell you said to my wife."

"I'm afraid that's not possible. Why don't you ask her?"

"I have and she told me to go to hell."

"I see."

"No, you don't see! I want to know what lies she's been telling you. I deserve to know."

"Actually, you do not. And, in truth, most of the conversation had nothing to do with you. I'd suggest that you drop it. People have a right to privacy, even married people."

"My wife's as much a whore as I am. Bet she didn't tell you that."

"Mr. Silverman, may I remind you that this is a homicide investigation. Do you have something useful you would like to contribute to finding the murderer, or murderers of Harry Winthrop or Ralph Boardman?"

"Certainly not, as you well know. What could I possibly know, which is why I demand to be allowed to go home!"

"Of course."

"Excuse me?"

"You and Ms. Drake are free to go. We have your address and one of my officers will accompany you home to take temporary possession of your passport."

"Over my dead body."

"Or, you can remain in residence here, indefinitely, until this case wraps up."

"This is preposterous. By what authority have you?"

"Judge Williams in Northport has already issued the warrant, and should you choose to depart, I have given Officer Pacheco in the local office the order. She will be happy to follow you home when you're ready."

At that moment, Tim Hargreaves interrupted them, a beer in hand. "Where's Lib?"

"Who the hell knows."

Hargreaves turned and rolled his eyes at Demaris. "Aren't we the testy one tonight. I was coming over to see if you want to take a run in the morning."

"Excuse me, gentlemen," Demaris said, turning to go.

Silverman replied in a voice much louder than necessary. "It will have to be an early one, 'cause we're out of here at nine sharp."

As Demaris waved over his shoulder, he heard Hargreaves say, "What was that about, bro?"

CHAPTER 49

Pete and Greta surveyed the crowd as their boss wove among them. Mourners were beginning to say their goodbyes and depart. "Should I go get him and remind him of the time," she said, checking her watch. It was just six and they promised Charlotte Lang that they would be there promptly at seven.

"Leave him a minute. Once he sees you, he'll come over. I expect he'll want you to stay until everyone leaves."

"Or you."

"I'm going with him."

"Has he said that?"

"No, but he doesn't have to."

"I just thought since it's a woman, he might want me to go."

"Well, we're about to find out," Dugan said, puffing out his chest as their boss approached.

"Anything new, Greta?"

"No, sir."

"Were you able to get photos?"

"No, but Stevens is on it. The only ones we found so far are really grainy, but he's digging. Has lots of Stella Lang, but not her siblings."

"Well, we're about to meet one. Perhaps she'll have pictures or a story to tell."

"Stevens says if he finds any pics, he'll e-mail them. I have the iPad in the car."

Pete cleared his throat. "We better get going, boss. It's six now."

Demaris turned and smiled at his second-in-command, knowing his next words would not be well-received. "I want you here, Pete."

"But, I—"

"This is too important. I need you watching everyone, making sure Mr. Winthrop and Ms. Dore are safe."

"What about Greta and the local guys? They can play babysitter just as well as I can."

Demaris turned to her. "Greta, would you pull the car around. I'll be right out. Okay?"

When Greta had closed the door behind her, he turned back and placed a firm hand on Pete's muscular forearm. "Listen to me. Anyone can sit in on an interview, and Greta is a woman, which helps. But, I only have one of you. I believe there is still significant danger here, to both Mr. Winthrop and Bess."

"Do you know something?"

"No, but I'm certain of it. Pete, I need you here, to watch over them. As soon as Stevens is finished, I've asked him to get in touch and you can put him where you think best."

"But, Rodge, I—"

"I've got to go. Looks like Ms. Dore needs rescuing right now from that lecherous former headmaster."

"Okay, maybe I'll go arrest Mr. Chips."

Demaris laughed. "That's the spirit. Thanks, Pete. Don't let her out of your sight."

"You mean them, don't you?"

With a deep, slow breath, he replied, "Yes, them. Stevens should stay here, after everyone departs. You go with Bess and Mrs. Guilford."

He watched Pete head for Bess and Peter Thurbert, then turned and slipped out the door.

As she made her way toward the far end of the room, hoping to intercept Jane, Bess bumped into Peter Thurbert. "Oh, Peter, I'm so sorry! I seem to be colliding with everyone tonight."

Almost a head taller than Bess, the former headmaster gazed down at her with genuine warmth. "No problem, I've been trying to see you for a couple of days. Your mother and Jane are formidable gatekeepers."

She laughed. "Yes, I expect they are. Sorry, but I was in no shape for visitors. Still not, but will collapse after today."

"I'm so sorry, my dear."

"Thank you. Are you okay? You don't look at all well, Peter."

They stood apart out of earshot of the other guests. "I've been better." He gave her a wan smile.

"Where's Carrie?"

"She went home after the service with a headache, or so she said. I imagine she's somewhere commiserating with Will McGuire."

Shocked, Bess stared up at her friend. Many on campus knew of Carrie Thurbert's affair with Will McGuire, upper school English teacher, but the general consensus was that her husband was still in the dark.

"Don't say anything. I can see by your expression that you know about Carrie and Will, but assumed I did not."

"I'm sorry."

"Don't be. I've known for years, but when I was carrying on with Jane it didn't matter. Jane and I broke it off a few months before I retired. I told Carrie I wanted to make a fresh start, make a go of our marriage so to speak. She agreed and said she'd end things with Will. That lasted about a week. Apparently they can't live without one another."

"Oh, Peter, how dreadful for you. What will you do?"

"I don't know. Divorce is more realistic now that I have no reputation to uphold. I hope you'll still be my friend, no matter what happens." He reached out and grasped her hands, massaging them gently, his expression making it plain the kind of friendship he desired.

Instantly, she withdrew her hands and stepped back. "Peter, I will always be your friend, but that's all. Nothing more. Please don't do this again."

"But, Bess, I—"

"Could I have a word, Ms. Dore?" She turned to find Pete Dugan behind her. "It's rather urgent, if you don't mind coming with me."

"Of course," she said, following Pete without another word to Peter Thurbert. "What is it?" she whispered as they reached a side door and stepped into the hallway.

When she looked up at him, Dugan was grinning. "Rodge sent me. Nothing's wrong, but he thought it looked as if you needed rescuing."

"Oh, Pete," she cried, hugging the startled Dugan. "You have no idea how much! Please thank him. Where is he?"

"He had to leave. I'm here to watch over things. Just give me a signal if you need me, okay?"

She nodded and headed for a circle of teachers that included Jane Fellows, Joan Nettlemen, and a few others.

As Pete headed for an inconspicuous spot at the edge of the crowd, he overheard Wolfson and Hargreaves, the former drunk as usual, ranting about how his companion had used his "poor Sophie."

"Everything okay, guys?" Pete said, stepping closer.

"Time to take Boyle home, Officer. As usual, he's drunk and making a scene."

"It's Detective, sir. Mr. Wolfson, would you like someone to take you back to your room?"

Wolfson peered at Pete through bloodshot eyes. It almost appeared that he had been crying. "No, I would like to have this asshole admit that he used my Sophie shamelessly."

"We were under the impression that she was no longer your Sophie, sir?"

"Thanks to him."

"Have you had recent contact with Ms. Calivera, Mr. Hargreaves?" "No, I have not. Haven't seen her since Madrid."

"Bullshit!"

Wolfson's voice carried and people stopped talking to stare. As Pete motioned to one of the local officers, Carrion Littlefield approached. "I'll take him back. Come on, Boyle, old boy."

"You're at the inn, though, aren't you, sir?"

"Yes, but I'll drop him off and see that he gets to his room, not to worry."

"That's considerate of you, but Officer Rego can accompany you, if you like."

"No, let me. You stay busy with your survailing. Is that a word, survailing? I like the sound of it."

Ignoring the question, Pete instructed Officer Rego to help them to the car and the men departed. Wolfson staggered and nearly fell into the cheese table on the way out.

"Pathetic," Hargreaves said as he and Pete watched. "Don't imagine his bookshop will stay afloat for much longer, do you?"

"Was there any truth to what he said about Ms. Calivera and you?"

"What'd you think, Detective?" the other said, lifting his beer bottle in toast and turning to join Bess and her fellow teachers. Pete noticed that as soon as he reached them, Bess took hold of Jane Fellows' arm and pulled her away, heading to find Maggie Guilford.

CHAPTER 50

Street venders hawking everything from pottery to velvet paintings were just closing up shop as Demaris and Greta parked and walked a block to the enormous granite building, a sign over the front entrance identifying it as "Artisans' Mill Lofts and Studios."

"This should be interesting," he said as they headed in. "Think we'll find looms whirring and cotton dust flying?"

She laughed, knowing her boss was kidding and simply trying to lighten the mood. "Hardly, boss. These are the most exclusive artist digs in the city. Very upscale, very expensive."

"How expensive?"

"Well, all the lofts are taken, but the last one sold for two million."

He whistled. "Far cry from the poor slaves who worked here a hundred years ago."

"It's kind of the new thing. To live and work in a place. Artists like Charlotte Lang need big spaces."

"She is?"

"Metal sculptress. Huge pieces, all over the city. She's been pretty successful here, and in Boston, and New York. That's probably one of hers." She pointed at a series of enormous panels of varying size and color suspended above them, punctuated by globe lights hanging around and among them.

After looking up, eying the piece for several minutes, he grinned. "Now I've gotta meet the artist."

When they reached the landing, they spied Charlotte Lang standing at the open door. It was a massive oak thing, at least ten feet tall, with elaborate carvings. Definitely not from the original mill.

His height, Lang's curly red hair was flecked with gray. Freckles splayed across her nose and rosy cheeks and bright blue eyes regarded them with curiosity and not a hint of guile. She was dressed in jeans and a torn tee shirt, rag wool socks and no shoes.

"Good evening, Ms. Lang, I'm Lieutenant Demaris and this is my colleague, Detective Burke. I believe she told you why we wanted to see you?"

"I believe you're right. This is a first for me."

"Visitors or a visit from the police?"

"Both. I'm kind of a hermit, but I do get the occasional visitor. Never a couple of homicide detectives though. Come in, can I get you something?"

"Thank you, we're fine," he said. "Might we sit down?"

"Of course." She led them into a vast room with two enormous sofas facing each other. They were covered in buttery suede that looked expensive, kilim pillows tossed haphazardly on each. Their hostess flopped down on one sofa and waved them into the other.

Demaris preferred sitting in straight-backed chairs for interviews, but took a seat on the opposite sofa, Greta several feet to his left. "Thank you for seeing us, Ms. Lang."

"Did I have a choice?"

She smiled, clearly toying with him. He gazed around the cavernous space, thinking how cold and stark it was, made even colder by the artist's creations scattered about on the floor, and hanging from the dark gray walls and tangerine ceiling. After a few seconds, where he tried to recall if he had ever seen paint in such a dramatic hue, he returned his gaze to their hostess.

"Interesting home you have, Ms. Lang. You must do very well with your artwork."

"Bought the loft three years ago, with my inheritance. I live very frugally, Detective. This is my one extravagance."

"What can you tell us about your brother, Julian? We've been trying to locate him and so far have been unsuccessful."

"My stepbrother, you mean? I haven't the faintest idea. We were never close."

"Oh?"

"My mother died when I was six and my father remarried Nina Fairfax almost immediately. I wouldn't be surprised if she'd had her eyes on him, ready to swoop in, the entire time my mom was ill."

"I'm sorry. She must have been young."

"Thirty-one. Breast cancer. It was a horrible six months."

He nodded, waiting for her to continue. "My mom came from a big Irish family, but after Dad married Nina we barely saw them."

"Were you an only child, before your father remarried?"

"Yes, my mom had miscarried a few times after me."

"So Stella Lang was a stepsister?"

She nodded. "Yes, I had one of each. A wicked stepbrother and stepsister. They were ten and twelve so they had no use for me except to torment me when they were bored."

"How so?"

"Oh, the usual deviant things—locking me in the basement, hiding my things, cutting the hair off my dolls, torturing my cat. Anything to see me cry."

"Didn't your parents intervene?"

"Surely you jest? Fortunately Stella and Julian were so locked in their own sick and tortured relationship that they ignored me most of the time."

"What was the nature of their relationship, if you don't mind my asking?"

"I haven't a clue, Detective. All I can tell you is that they disappeared into Stella's bedroom every night and didn't emerge till morning. When she died, he locked himself up in there for over a month, only opening the door when Cook brought food."

"That must have been terrible."

She shrugged. "What would have been terrible is if my dad had died before Nina. If he had, I'm sure she would have found some nefarious way to divert his entire estate away from me, leaving it all to her precious Julian. It was Dad's money, you see.

"As it was, her beloved Julian's behavior after Stella's death brought home the truth about their sordid, secret relationship and Nina died of grief or revulsion a month before my dad so Julian and I split the estate, as my father had intended. Nina worshipped Stella, but she adored Julian. His betrayal destroyed her."

"What was the cause of death of your father and stepmother?"

"Our family physician, a quack if there ever was one, said that Nina died of complete organ failure due to grief. My dad had a heart attack, but he had been sick for a number of weeks before he died."

"Was he close to your stepsiblings?"

"Not particularly, but he took good care of them for Nina's sake."

"Had she been ill before her death?"

"Hard to say since she was a total hypochondriac. Always complaining about her delicate constitution. After Julian emerged from Stella's bedroom, Nina took to her bed and rarely got up or went out. It was all for attention, if you ask me. Had poor, contrite Julian waiting on her hand and foot. Toward the end the only thing she'd eat were the disgusting green smoothies he whipped up for her."

"I see. Were your parents laid to rest with your stepsister?"

"No, all three of them were cremated. Nina kept Stella's ashes and Julian scattered both of them in the Charles River less than a week after Nina died, why?"

"What about your father?"

"Right there," she said, pointing to a large metal urn perched on one of the rungs of a metal staircase-like structure that ran from floor to ceiling. "Julian wanted to scatter him with Nina, but I refused. He was quite miffed. Actually, that's the last time I laid eyes on my dear stepbrother."

"Might you have a photo of your brother anywhere?"

"Are you kidding? I wouldn't keep a picture of him or his hideous lover anywhere in my home."

"Was he blonde like you stepsister?"

"Stella's hair color came out of a bottle, Detective. Or, more accurately, the laboratory of her stylist to whom she shelled out a thousand dollars every two weeks. Both of them were dark-haired, brown, I'd guess, although Stella went back and forth between brunette and blonde since her early teens. For all I know, Julian colored his hair, too."

"Ms. Lang, I have what might seem like an odd request."

"Yes?"

"Might I borrow your father's ashes, just for a short time? I promise they will be returned to you intact."

"Do you think my father might have been murdered?"

"I don't know, but I'd like to have the ashes tested."

She stared from him to Greta, lower lip trembling. After several minutes, she said, "Okay, yes, go ahead. You can take the urn, or if you lift the lid, the bag inside comes out."

He gave Greta a look and she pulled a thick evidence bag from her pocket. "The bag will be fine. We'll take good care of it."

She nodded, tears shining in her bright eyes. "He was all I had, my dad."

"Yes, I'm sorry."

"If it's true, will you tell me?"

"Of course." Demaris rose, watching as Greta carefully lifted the plastic bag of ashes from the urn and zipped it into the evidence sack. "Thank you for your time, Ms. Lang."

She walked them to the door and watched from the landing as they headed down the winding stairs. "Detectives," she called, as they reached the ground floor. "If it's true and you find the bastard, tell him I hope he rots in hell."

They made their way along the now deserted sidewalk in silence until they reached the car. "What have we walked into, sir?"

He shook his head. "We'll leave these with Megan, then get back to the village as soon as we can."

Megan was waiting when they arrived. "Do you want to wait, sir?" she said, her assistant standing at her side.

"No, we've gotta run. Call me the second you know something."

CHAPTER 51

They had just pulled out of the clinic lot when Greta's iPad dinged. Greta was driving so she said, "You better look, sir. It's probably from Stevens."

"Pull over, then. I don't want to wrangle with the thing for ten minutes."

She drew up to the curb and stopped, taking the iPad from him. With a few clicks, accessed her e-mail finding three messages from Stevens. The first displayed a shot of Nina Lang and her husband, Charlotte's father, emerging from a church. The caption, identified the occasion as Stella Lang's funeral. The second photo accompanied the announcement of Stella's engagement to Harry Winthrop Junior. They were both smiling, but neither looked particularly happy. Stella Lang reminded him of someone, but he couldn't place the face. The last e-mail was a grainy shot of a man and a woman. "That's Charlotte, isn't it?" Greta said, pointing to her. "And, oh my God, is that who I think it is?" The caption read: "Charlotte and Julian Lang, children of the late Nina and Charles Lang."

Demaris grabbed the iPad. "Jesus Christ, let's go."

As Greta drove, he dialed Pete's cell over and over but it went straight to voicemail, the same with Stevens. When he tried the Old Harbor Police station, the desk clerk told him everyone had gone home, except Officer Rego, who was supposedly with Pete Dugan. When he tried Rego, his phone went to voice mail, too.

"Can't you go any faster?"

"Not if we want to get there, sir."

Chapter 52

Brendan Stevens had just sent the three e-mails to Greta's iPad when the door opened. "Oh, it's you," he said. "I just sent a photo of you to the Lieutenant."

He didn't see the rag until it was slapped over his face and darkness overtook him.

Pete Dugan waited with Officer Rego until all the mourners had departed the Winthrop estate. He left Rego with the old man with strict instructions not to let anyone into his room, after which he followed Bess and her mother's car home and escorted them into the house.

"This really isn't necessary, Pete," Bess said. "We're fine now. Go home, get some rest."

"Orders are orders. I'm going to be in my car, in your driveway until Rodge gets back."

"Well, that's ridiculous."

"I think it's very gallant," Maggie Guilford said, patting Pete on the cheek. "Thank you, Peter, dear. I feel much safer under your watchful eye."

"Goodnight, then."

As he stepped off the stoop, Dugan heard them lock the front door behind him. Unfortunately, he failed to see the bat as it swung out and knocked him senseless and bleeding on the gravel drive.

Ten minutes later, Bess and Maggie sat in the study with mugs of chamomile tea, when a knock at the front door startled them.

Bess looked at her mother. "Now what could he want? There's a reason Roger calls him a Mother Hen."

At that moment, the phone rang. "You get that and I'll see what Pete wants."

Maggie Guilford answered, listened and dropped the phone, crying out to her daughter, "Bess, wait, don't open it!" but she was too late. When she reached the front door, her daughter was gone and Pete Dugan lay on the drive, blood streaming from the side of his head.

She screamed and rushed back to the phone where Demaris waited. "What's happened? Where is she?"

"Gone, oh, Roger, she's gone and Pete, he's in the driveway. Oh, Roger, he's—"

"We'll be there in five minutes. Call an ambulance, Maggie. Now!"

CHAPTER 53

"What's happened, sir?" Greta asked, gazing over at her superior, his face drained of color.

He shook his head. "Where would he go?" For all he knew, Pete was dead and she would be, too, if they didn't think and act swiftly.

"He has them?"

"Bess, he has Bess and Pete's badly hurt or worse."

They pulled up the cottage driveway just ahead of the ambulance and he rushed to his assistant's side, leaning down to listen to his chest. Dugan's breath came in short gasps, but his heart had a steady beat.

"Thank God, he's alive. Pete, stay with us now, do you hear me?"

In answer, Dugan's eyes fluttered open. "I'm sorry, Rodge," he whispered, then closed his eyes and lapsed into unconsciousness.

The EMTs stood by with the stretcher. "Let us take him, now, sir."

Tears rimmed his eyes as Demaris stood and watched them lift Pete onto the stretcher. Greta stood nearby, tears snaking down her cheeks. The sight of her distress jolted him and he shook himself. "He's in good hands. We have to act fast. Where the hell would he take her? What's he drive?"

"A dark green Jag."

CHAPTER 54

As they stepped into the inn's lobby, they spied Tim Hargreaves and Liz Reynolds in the left parlor, sifters of brandy in hand. At that moment, Demaris' phone rang. "Bess, is that you? Where are you?"

Motioning to Greta, he stepped back outside, leaving Tim and Liz, mouths agape.

Listening carefully, he recognized the sound of an engine, a Jaguar engine. "Where are you? Can you talk? You can't talk? See if you can get him to say where he's taking you."

As he spoke, he and Greta hopped into the car. "Get ready. As soon as we know something, we've gotta go." She started the engine and he pressed his ear to the phone, straining to hear her above the Jag's roar.

Still groggy, Bess groaned and mumbled, "Where am I?"

"Relax, Ms. Dore. We'll be there soon."

"Where are you taking me?"

"One of your favorite spots, remember? Where you and dear Harry would go to gaze out at the sea, fondling each other, planning your future. A future my sister will never have."

"You mean Osprey Point?" she asked, wondering how he had known Harry and she loved to go there.

"Osprey Point," Demaris whispered. "Hurry, Burke. They've had a good head start."

"Patience, my dear. Don't want to give everything away."

"Why are we going to the Point?"

"It's a sad story, my dear. About a despondent fiancée who could go on without her beloved. I mean, how many men can you lose without wanting to end it all? Yes, I'm 'fraid you throw yourself off the cliff. Too bad that bumbling detective isn't here to save you. Where is he anyway? He's in love with you, by the way. Did you know that?"

"Why are you doing this?"

Demaris listened as sounds changed and he realized the Jag had left the paved road and had begun its climb across the bumpy field that led to the Point. "Stall him, Bess. Do anything you have to do, but stall him. Hold on to the seat. Don't leave the car if you can help it."

Suddenly, the line went dead and he remembered that once on the Point, cell phone reception died.

They raced along the dark coast road, covering the five miles in record time. As Greta turned onto the grass, their headlights caught the two of them as he dragged her toward the cliff. Greta drove as far as she could, then he jumped out and broke into a run.

"Littlefield, let her go! It's over."

"Go to hell," he cried as he dragged Bess to the cliff's edge. She tried to fight, but it was clear she was still weak and groggy. Greta had her gun trained at Littlefield, but dared not shoot.

"Listen to me, Carrion. Bess Dore has done nothing to you. This is craziness. Let her go, come back with us."

He laughed, yanking Bess' arm back behind her. "Now who's crazy?"

"Let her go. We can help you. We've spoken to Charlotte. We know how much you loved Stella."

Stunned, Littlefield paused, relaxing his grip on her arm and she kicked him, pulling free and running toward them. As he straightened, he pulled a gun from his coat and aimed, just as Greta fired, hitting him squarely in the chest. In the glare of the headlights, they saw a look of surprise on the slender, handsome face as he fell back and disappeared over the edge. At that moment, Bess reached him, throwing herself into his arms.

"You're okay, you're safe," he whispered, holding her tightly.

Burke advanced toward the cliff, training her powerful flashlight over the edge, where Carrion Littlefield's body lay on the sand, gentle waves nudging the sleeves of his four-thousand-dollar suit.

Chapter 55

Maggie Guilford and Jane Fellows met them at the hospital. "Take good care of her," he whispered, handing her over to their care. They nodded and headed inside, the nurses trailing alongside them.

Demaris grabbed one of the EMTs, who was headed back out. "My officer? Pete Dugan? How is he?"

"Not sure, sir. They took him upstairs right away."

Demaris pulled out his card and handed it to him. "Do me a favor and bring this in before you go? Tell 'em I want to be called right away."

The man nodded and headed back into the Emergency Room.

They found Officer Rego gagged and bound in his squad car with a nasty lump on the back of his head. No one in the Winthrop household had heard anything. A small case in Littlefield's glove box held a syringe, which they surmised he meant for Harry Winthrop Senior, once his future daughter-in-law had been dispatched.

Brendan Stevens had awakened and managed to loosen his bindings. He met them at the estate and was now standing guard at the front door. "Everybody's safe, sir."

"Good work, Stevens. I want you out here all night, but let's ask Molly Pierce or Helen to let you in. No sense standing out here in the cold."

Before they could knock, the housekeeper opened the front door and ushered Stevens in. As they turned away, Demaris patted the young man's shoulder. "Good work, Brendan. One of the best decisions I made this week, asking you to join us." Stevens blushed crimson and smiled at them both. "Thank you, sir."

"We're headed back to the hospital. Thanks for putting my officer up, Ms. Stevens."

"We are grateful for his presence," she said, nodding and closing the door softly behind them.

Pete was covered with apparatus, his red hair peeking through the bandage that covered his head. He appeared to be sleeping when they arrived. The moment he saw him, Demaris' eyes filled with tears. As he approached the bed, Greta quietly stepped back into the hall.

He pulled up a chair and sat quietly, watching the monitors, then his assistant sleeping soundly. As the machines hissed and beeped, he reached forward and rested his hand on Pete's arm, reminding himself to breathe.

What would he do without Pete? How could he have been so stupid as to leave him alone? He should have had the whole local force backing him up, but instead he let his stupid pride get in the way. His foolish need to show the world that his team could do it alone, that they were invincible had led to so many mistakes, including almost getting this young man he loved killed. Idiot, idiot, idiot, became his mantra as he sat watching Pete. He had internalized the mindfulness' quality of nonjudgmental present moment awareness much of the time, but at this moment it was a struggle.

A few minutes later a nurse appeared. "Are you a relative?"

"Yes," he replied, lying.

"Are you his dad?"

"Uncle. His dad's dead. How is he?"

"He's a very lucky young man. Serious concussion, but doctor expects him to make a full recovery. Hard-headed, that's what Doc Raymond says."

Demaris smiled. "Yes, he is that."

As he turned back, Pete opened his eyes and mumbled.

"He's heavily sedated so I doubt he'll make much sense."

After checking the various machines and tubes running into her patient, she turned to go. "No heavy conversations, no upsetting him. He needs to rest."

"Hey, Pete, how're you doing?"

"I'm sorry, Rodge. Is she? Did he?"

"She's safe. You did great buddy."

Pete gave him a goofy smile and closed his eyes.

Later, he stepped outside the room where Greta waited, two cups of coffee in her hands, one of which she handed to him.

"Greta, I'm gonna stay here tonight. Can you check on Ms. Dore, then go back and get some sleep?"

"Already did, sir. She's fine. Her mom and Ms. Fellows took her home."

"Get some sleep, then."

"Megan just called. Ashes full of arsenic. He killed that poor woman's dad."

"Yes." He nodded, started to turn away, then called after her. "Greta?"

"Yes, sir?"

"If anyone asks, I'm his uncle."

"I already confirmed that, sir."

"Good work tonight. Thank you."

CHAPTER 56

Ralph Boardman's service was held at nine Tuesday morning at the tiny Baptist Church the Boardmans had joined shortly after arriving in Old Harbor. There were about two dozen mourners, relatives, a few villagers, and the Winthrop household. Bess came with Peter Thurbert, no Carrie in sight. Arthur Burnham joined them in the pew. It was a simple stone-and-wood structure with clear glass-leaded windows and oak pews with floral carvings at each end. The day was cool and overcast when they arrived, but soon the sun came out, its light warming the cold, dark space.

The service lasted just over thirty minutes with the pastor's words then readings from Charlie Boardman and a young woman, a cousin, who appeared to be about his age. As the mourners filed out, Demaris found Bess in a tiny group that included Mr. Winthrop Senior, who sat in a wheelchair flanked by Molly Pierce and Helen Stevens. Brendan Stevens stood ten feet away, still on duty and Bess and Peter Thurbert stood to the side.

"Good morning, sir," the elder Winthrop called as he approached. "Well done. Brendan did a heroic, but unnecessary job as watchdog last night. Please excuse my wheels. My self-appointed nurses insisted I travel this way."

Demaris nodded to the others, his eyes lingering on Bess slightly longer than her companions, then smiled and took a seat on a bench beside the wheelchair. "Very wise of them. Yes, I think we can relieve your guard now." He waved to Stevens, who hurried over. "Good work, Officer Stevens. Time for you to go home and get some sleep."

"I can stay, sir."

The young officer looked as if he might nod off standing up. How many days had it been since he slept? Demaris wondered. "No need. Danger over. Go home. The team will meet this afternoon at three to wrap up and clean out the guest house. Come then, if you can."

Stevens nodded, clearly reluctant to go, but finally headed to his car.

Demaris turned back to the old man. "He was a good man."

"Yes, he was. Wish the son would stay on."

"Probably too many memories." He gazed from Winthrop to the two women who had accompanied him. Molly nodded, eyes filled with tears. The housekeeper bowed her head, but said nothing. "My team closes up shop today. Can we do anything for you before we leave town?"

"I suspect we'll muddle along. Franklin and D'Angelis, my attorneys, will be down tomorrow to fuss over me so I won't be too lonely."

Despite his bravado, his voice trembled and Harry Winthrop Senior appeared to have aged twenty years. As Demaris watched him, he marveled again at the man's resiliency. "I'm sorry, sir."

"For what?"

"If we'd moved faster, asked the right questions, we'd have uncovered the link between Julian Lang, aka Carrion Littlefield and Ralph."

"I never met the man."

"No, but Ralph had. He knew Julian. So, Julian had to kill him, and quickly."

"So, it wasn't because Ralph saw him the day of Harry's death?" Peter Thurbert asked.

"No, he worked for the Lang family, Julian, or Carrion's parents," Demaris said. "Came to the Winthrops after the parents died."

"He was Stella's brother," Bess said.

"Never liked her, cold fish," Winthrop muttered. "Ladies, take me home please."

Molly waved to Charlie Boardman, who was driving them home. Charlie had agreed to fill in part-time at the estate until they could find a replacement for his father. Demaris stood and shook Harry Winthrop's hand.

"Don't be a stranger, Lieutenant. Come and see an old man if you're in the village."

"Count on it, sir," he said, as he helped Molly to disengage the wheelchair brakes.

As they made their way toward the car, he wondered if he would ever see the bright-eyed, sharp-tongued octogenarian again. Peter Thurbert stood near the car, waiting. As Mr. Winthrop was assisted into his black Cadillac, Bess patted her former boss' arm.

"Peter, thanks for bringing me. I think I'll walk home."

"I can walk with you and come back for my car."

"I'm fine, really. You go. I'd like to sit here for a bit."

As she sat, Demaris turned to face the retired headmaster. "Good to see you again, Thurbert. Take care."

Thurbert nodded to Bess, then him. "Well, then, I'll be off."

Once they were alone, the two sat side by side on a stone bench overlooking the village green.

"How are you?"

"Numb. How's Pete?"

"He'll be fine. Hard head, big scar."

"Poor guy."

"Yes. Bess, I'm sorry."

"Me, too."

"I'm talking about Harry."

"I know. I'm am, too, but not just Harry."

"You're right, not just Harry."

He reached over and took her hand in his, and they sat in the silence of late morning, the church bells tolling for Ralph Boardman.

EPILOGUE

The team assembled for the last time at the guest house, Tilly's sandwiches and a huge bag of cookies from Lois and Cathy spread out before them. Demaris' things were already packed in the jeep, ready to head home, but he hated to go, to leave his people or the village, which held so much of his heart.

Pete had insisted upon coming with the promise that he would return to the hospital for one more night of observation after they were through. Greta picked him up. He was a bit wobbly on his feet, but his blue eyes were clear.

"How did he know so much about Harry and Bess and their habits? Like the trips to Osprey Point?" he asked.

"Littlefield, or Lang, hired a private investigator, who's been following them for months. Amazing that no one in the village noticed him," Greta said, shaking her head. It was clear she was anxious to go. Throughout the packing up, she had fielded a number of phone calls, presumably about her mother. The temporary caregiver had finally had enough.

"Why?"

As he spoke, Pete fingered the bandage still wrapped around his head. The doctor had told Demaris that there would be a large scar and suggested that plastic surgery might be necessary down the road. He had lost a lot of blood and his normally pale skin was ashen.

"Harry Winthrop stole his lover, then killed her."

"Lover?"

Greta smiled, regarding her colleague, her gaze reflecting the same concern of her boss. "You missed a bit of the story, Pete. I'll fill you in on our way back to the hospital. Maybe we'd better head out? What do you say?"

"I'm totally fine."

"No, you're not. We're done. You go with Greta. Brendan and I will take care of this stuff."

"But—"

"That's an order, Dugan. Now, beat it. Again, good work, everyone."

"What about you, sir?" she said, grasping Pete's elbow as they headed for the door.

"I'm gonna stop at the Clinic and check in with Megan before she closes up shop. Wanna make sure Charlotte Lang gets her dad's ashes back, too. After that, I'll head home."

"No other stops?" Pete asked.

Demaris stared at his assistant, insubordinate as always. "Not today, Mother Hen. Now, get out of here."

Stevens helped dispose of the trash and gather the remaining folders into a box, which he packed into Demaris' car. When he returned, his superior was sitting quietly at the empty table. "Is that all, sir?"

"Have you got a few minutes, Brendan?"

"Of course, sir."

"Sit, then."

When they were face to face, he looked up at the young officer and smiled warmly. "You did very good work, Brendan."

"Thank you, sir."

"You have skills they can't teach at the academy. The skills that are invaluable to a team like ours."

"Excuse me, sir?"

"You listen, read people, and seem to be able to ferret out almost anything on the Internet."

"Thank you, sir."

"If I'd set you loose the day Winthrop was killed, we may have saved Ralph Boardman's life."

"But?"

He raised his hand. "No, that's my problem, not yours. I wanted to ask if you would have interest in working on R.H.D. on a permanent basis? Detectives Burke and Dugan would be your immediate supervisors most of the time. If you accept, I would ask them to train you. Would you think about it?"

"I don't have to think about it, sir. It would be my honor to work for you."

He smiled. "Even so, think about it. If you're sure in a day or two, let me know and I'll speak to Chief Wilbur, okay?"

"Yes, sir. I will, sir."

"Okay, now go home and get some rest. You look like shit."

Stevens could not stop grinning as he stood, collected his jacket, and headed out with several more "thank you, sirs" on his way to the door.

When he was alone, Demaris looked around the empty room and shook his head. Stevens and Greta had let the weekend guests know they were free to go. As he sat in the silence, his cell phone rang and he saw Bess' name.

"Hello?"

"Roger, I, my mother wants to speak with you. Would that be okay?"

He assented and almost immediately heard Maggie Guilford's voice. "Roger, I could not go home tomorrow without saying goodbye and thank you for saving my precious daughter's life."

"Glad we could be there."

"No, I want to say this, Roger. Please listen. I may have misjudged you, and if I have, I'm sorry."

"No apology necessary, Ms. Guilford."

"Maggie, please. And, I disagree. I was terrible to you all those years ago and not much better for most of this week."

"I'm not the easiest person, Maggie. Let's leave it at that."

"Well, I do hope to see you next time I'm in Old Harbor. Take care, and here's my daughter."

Bess came on and asked him to hold. "Hi, wanted to get out of earshot. Sorry about that."

He laughed. "Stranger things have happened, but I can't think what they are at this moment."

"I hope you'll come back and visit soon."

"Thanks. This might sound weird, but I was going to ask, if you're not busy for Thanksgiving, whether you might like to spend it with Mary, the kids, and me."

"That's very kind, but I've agreed to fly down and be with Mother and Tim. Will be good to get away for a few days. Even if I was here, I'm not sure it's the best time? I would hate to make Mary uncomfortable when you're just getting to know Owen and all."

"Maybe not, but didn't want you to be alone. Maybe we'll invite Harry Winthrop Senior and his household?"

She laughed. "I believe Ralph's sister, Charlie's Aunt Jean has already swooped in with a Thanksgiving plan."

"Well, enjoy the holiday."

"Will I see you before long?"

"Count on it," he said, quietly. "Take care of yourself, Bess."

"You, too."

Please read on to preview chapters from Lee's mystery, *Lost in Spindle City*, book three in the *Ricky Steele Mystery* series!

ACKNOWLEDGEMENTS

Thank you to my friend and neighbor, Sgt. Jason Pacheco of the Fall River, Massachusetts Police Department, for talking with me about police procedures, and especially about the idea of a regional homicide division. Any misunderstandings in this area are entirely mine as he is always very clear and professional.

Always, I thank my dear family and friends, who are there, no matter where life's travels take me. I love them all beyond words. A special thanks to sister, Pamela, for her proofreading. No matter how many edits, we still find typos!

Grateful appreciation goes to the Formatting Fairies, and the unfailing good cheer and encouragement they bestow upon this fledgling author. Special thanks to Ashley Lopez for designing the lovely covers that encourage readers to pick up each book! And, of course, a huge thank you to my readers for picking up my books, for writing to tell me you love them, and for continuing to come back for more. It is heartwarming to know you are out there!

Author's Note

This book, setting and characters are dear to me. I love writing about village life and the flawed, very human Roger Demaris. *In the Name of Silence* is the second mystery featuring Bess Dore and Roger Demaris. Many authors have a favorite character, and, I must confess, Ricky Steele (of the Ricky Steele series) is mine, however, in Roger Demaris I have found what may be a Ricky's equal.

If you liked *In the Name of Silence* and would be willing to write an Amazon review, I would very much appreciate it! In fact, I will be happy to send my first 25 reviewers a free e- copy of **another of my titles**! If you submit a review, just e-mail me at mleeprescott@gmail.com and I will see that you receive your free copy of whichever title you would like!

If you would like to sign up for future book releases and occasional notices about my books, please e-mail me at mleeprescott@gmail.com and I will add you to the list. I promise I will not share your address, nor will I flood you with e-mails. Do visit my website at www.mleeprescott.com to read more about my books and to hear what's next. I am really excited by my upcoming **Morgan's Run** series, set in the incredible United States southwest, another special place I visit often. First Morgan's Run title is scheduled for release in 2015!

Finally, this book has been revised, proofed and edited many, many times, but I, and my intrepid assistants, are human so if you spot a typo, please e-mail me at mleeprescott@gmail.com and I will fix it. If you'd like to know more about my other books, please scroll ahead to the next section that is followed by sample chapters of *Lost in Spindle City.*

Warm wishes,
M. Lee Prescott

ABOUT THE AUTHOR

M. Lee Prescott is the author of dozens of works of fiction for adults, young adults and children, among them mysteries, **Prepped to Kill, Gadfly, Lost in Spindle City (Ricky Steele series), Jigsaw, A Friend of Silence,** and romances, **Widow's Island** and **Hestor's Way**. Recently, her novel **Song of the Spirit** was made a finalist in the *2014 International Digital Awards* for young adult historical fiction. Her newest contemporary romance series, **Morgan's Run,** debuts in the summer of 2015. Three of her nonfiction titles have been published by Heinemann and she has published numerous articles in the field of literacy education. Lee is a professor of education at a small New England liberal arts college where she teaches reading and writing pedagogy. Her current research focuses on mindfulness and connections to reading and writing. She regularly teaches abroad, most recently in Singapore.

Lee has lived in southern California (loved those Laguna nights!), Chapel Hill, North Carolina, and various spots in Massachusetts, and Rhode Island. Currently, she resides in Massachusetts on a beautiful river, where she canoes, swims, and watches the incredible variety of migratory birds that pass by. She is the mother of two grown sons and spends lots of time with them, their beautiful wives, and her amazing grandchildren. When not teaching or writing (both of which she loves), Lee's passions revolve around family, yoga (Kripalu is a second home), swimming, sharing mindfulness with children and adults, and walking.

Lee loves to hear from readers. Visit her website at mleeprescott.com and Facebook page (mleeprescott). The Facebook page is a "work in progress," but I am working on it with help from friends who know what they are doing! E-mail is *mleeprescott@gmail.com*.

Contemporary romances and mysteries by M. Lee Prescott include:

Mysteries

The Ricky Steele series
Book 1: Prepped to Kill
Book 2: Gadfly
Book 3: Lost in Spindle City

Also featuring Ricky Steele:
Jigsaw

Single titles

Romantic suspense

Roger and Bess Mysteries
Book 1: A Friend of Silence
Book 2: In the Name of Silence (coming in April 2015!)

Contemporary Romance
Well Loved Series: Lassitor's Return (coming soon!)
Glass Walls (coming soon!)
Morgan's Run

Young Adult Historical Romance
Song of the Spirit

EXCERPT FROM LOST IN SPINDLE CITY
CHAPTER 1

Some days have less than auspicious starts. This was one of them. My third-floor office seemed light years away as I dragged myself up the stairs. My head was fuzzy, legs wet noodles, and my stomach churning. Other than that, I felt terrific.

Last night was one of the truly dumb ones where I forgot that I'm fifty-eight not twenty-eight. I had just wrapped up a crappy case, and despite my best efforts to breathe deeply and let go, my shoulders and neck were locked tight as a tick. Instead of taking a bath and hitting the sack, yours truly had to play tough PI, belting back beers with the guys at the *Rainbow*.

A little hole in the wall bar frequented by the locals, the *Rainbow* is a block from my house. A small cardboard sigh taped to the inside of the grimy front window, "Food and Spirits, do drop in," is the only indication that it's a place of business. The sign, brown and curling at the edges, was penned in red. The ink, now faded, coordinated nicely with the grayish pink, peek-a-boo, half curtains, frayed and dusty, after many smoky years. One glimpse of its subterranean façade and no passer-by would dare "to drop in."

Once I got started on the beers and shots of tequila, it was all over. My neighbor, Vinnie and I played cribbage or maybe dice. There used to be an ancient pool table, but Jack, the owner, had it removed the previous year, fearing its imminent collapse might injure one of his valued patrons.

The walk home, a dim memory, I had slept in my clothes—never a good sign. I woke at 6:00 a.m. and the phrase "death warmed over" sprang to mind. After three aspirins, a shower, juice and muffins, I felt better, but that's not saying much.

I'm supposed to have oat bran and lots of fiber to combat high cholesterol and triglycerides, but after ingesting platters of grease and empty carbs the previous evening, that was pretty much a losing battle.

A run? Out of the question. My daily yoga? Probably not wise to invert my body at present. Better to wait until dark to see stars. Maybe a short walk, then I'd treat myself to a coffee cab. The rest of the world calls them milkshakes, but around Spindle City, we call 'em cabs or cabinets. Yum!

I hate coffee, am a tea drinker, mostly Earl Grey and Yerba Mate, but I love coffee cabs and occasionally coffee ice cream, both of which serve as my primary treatment for the occasional hangover I experience as a middle-aged nincompoop. I keep a coffee maker in my office for clients and I've been known to swill a cup to be friendly, but coffee has never been part of my daily routine.

My name is Ricky Steele, given name, Dorothy. I've been married, but no kids, have one sister and a father who I see once in a while. I was married for about five seconds and have no children, the latter my one regret. I recently had, what for me, was a serious relationship that lasted about five months. It ended when he went back to his former live-in girlfriend. I had a history with Jay Harp, the lothario in question, and should have known better than to trust my heart to him again. We had a brief fling in our twenties when we were both members of a wedding party. As best man and maid of honor, we spent many hours together and one thing led to another. We kept things up for a month or two post-wedding, but then Jay disappeared, never to be seen again, until last year.

I was investigating the murder of his brother, Ron Harp when Jay and I met up again, and our former spark turned into a blaze. We spent some passionate, intense months with one another, and even discussed moving in together. Then Jay confessed that he had "unfinished business" with his former fiancée, Marty. What is it with men and "unfinished business" with old girlfriends? My reaction to his confession was to storm off and refuse to see him or talk to him. We speak on the phone every so often, but I always refuse to see him. I have to admit that I miss him. Our break-up hurt more than previous ones. My friends tell me I have a gift for choosing men who are dishonest and narcissistic, but maybe I'm not "girlfriend material?" Who knows? I try to stay positive and hope that the right guy will walk into my life someday.

I hold many odd jobs, from newspaper columnist for our local paper, to waitress and craftsperson. Most recently, I've been working as a private investigator, a profession, which I recently fell into thanks to my own foolishness. Then, to my surprise, I found I liked it enough to put in the hundreds of hours interning with two local PIs that were required in order to get my license. I'm a private person and this life suits my personality, if not my overall health, and I've let some of the odd jobs go, waitressing, in particular.

While I've stumbled into several murder cases, most of my work is fairly routine. A good friend, Bud Dixon, runs his own insurance business and throws me a fair amount of work. Insurance fraud is a full-time occupation for lots of folks so Bud's jobs help make ends meet. I also pick up a fair amount of work trailing errant spouses, since infidelity is epidemic. About half of this work is accomplished in the real world, the other half online, since the Internet is a cheater's best friend.

Over the past months, I've become the PI of choice for a certain Newport set. Having hubby followed and photographed as he goes about his tedious daily routines seems to be the "in thing" for bored housewives and those who have a vested interest in keeping close tabs on the checkbook.

My last case, which I tried mightily to stay out of, nearly got me killed. There are certain cases one does not take in this city, if one wishes to remain among the living. I was out of physical danger now, or at least for the next decade, but I was still emotionally shaken, hence last night's idiocy. I'm not a big drinker, the occasional beer and glass of wine is about the extent of it, but sometimes the amnesia of alcohol can be therapeutic. A day spent indulging myself with junk food and sugar and I'd be ready to face the world again.

As I reached the top of the stairs, my stomach flipped. Increased heart rate, beer and tequila definitely do not mix.

My office is in a restored mill building in the heart of the city's Flint District. It's a beautiful structure, the façade still strong and proud, despite acres of advertising splayed across its granite walls. In the city's hay day, its cavernous rooms once roared with the machinery of textile production, hundreds of workers toiling twenty-four hours a day. For years, the abandoned mill had sat, guttered and empty, left to ponder its fate as the once thriving city slipped into poverty, neglect and high unemployment. Now, although silent, the halls and passageways had been "repurposed" and housed a variety of enterprises.

The ground floor hummed with a ragtag collection of outlet stores and bargain kiosks hawking every type of merchandise, but right now the second floor is vacant, providing a buffer between Outlet Central and offices on the third floor. Bud, my insurance friend, began his business here and dragged me along, but as his client list grew, he moved to fancier digs downtown, leaving me with several other tenants on the partially renovated third floor. Not exactly a classy location, but it suits me. I have my own rear entrance, insulated from the comings and goings of the outlet crowd.

At the moment, there are four of us on the third floor. I'm in 308, a real estate appraiser I rarely see is in 312, a salesman for "Boats Afloat" or some nautical magazine is in 316. The writer in 320 comes most days at 10:00 a.m. and departs shortly before 3:00 p.m. He told me last week that 320 is his sanctuary, an escape from the bedlam at home. The remainder of the floor is vacant. An acre of empty is a lot of empty. They tell us there are sixty to eighty potential office spaces, but it takes a certain type to locate here. Cheap and bizarre. It's relatively quiet and fairly secure, at least during the day since they've hired extra security to keep the bargain hunter's thievery in check. Apparently for some, no price is cheap enough.

I slid open the heavy metal fire door and headed down the hall. The walls were painted dull, asylum grey, but they left the beautiful woodwork alone. I ran my hand along the dark mahogany chair rail, collecting dust. Unfortunately, the renovators had made no attempt to match the old with the new, so my cubicle and others had been slapped together, minus mahogany trim.

As a middle-aged spinster set in her ways, I have a little routine I like to follow which involves a cup of tea, a little bill paying, or ignoring, depending upon the status of my bank account, a little office tidying, record keeping, and whatever puttering I find to occupy me until I drink my tea. I do not like to be interrupted before 11:00 a.m. I have found this ritual to be important to my sense of well-being and willingness to face the day. I was not to enjoy my treasured routine today.

Chapter 2

I found her curled up against my door, a tangle of arms and legs. Her spindly legs were covered in snagged black netting that had been patched in several spots with nail polish. Bright red pumps, from all appearances, several sizes too large, adorned impossibly long feet.

Street people often camp out in buildings when they can slip by the airtight security system. In other words, they're regulars. I've kind of adopted one little lady, Irene, whom I suspect is around my age, but looks to be about a hundred. She's been sleeping in my hall for the past six months. If I forget to lock the office door, I often find her stretched out on my couch, catching up on her beauty sleep. Irene snores. Loudly. She's short and pudgy, not scrawny like this little gal with her bony limbs sticking out all over the place. I definitely did not have room on my couch for two.

I was contemplating how I might slip around my slumbering guest, when Terry, the appraiser, banged open the fire door and startled her awake. I turned to give him an icy glare, but he had already banged into his office, not a glance in our direction. Turning back, I found her rubbing her eyes, looking disoriented and none too happy. That made two of us.

She gathered herself up and ineffectually endeavored to smooth her hair as she inched up the wall like a spider. Her light brown hair, the consistency of my childhood dolls after I'd styled their tresses, stuck up in odd clumps, coarse, wiry and clearly in need of a wash. She wore a red skirt and matching ribbed top, the entire ensemble made of a hundred percent unnatural fibers. Over her skimpy get-up, she wore an oversized man's gray sport coat in a herringbone pattern, brown suede patches on the sleeves. I suspect she had grabbed it from the outlet dumpster on her way in, to ward off the April chill.

Several strands of brightly colored beads hung from her skinny, ostrich neck, and she sported matching dangly earrings. Her left earring was missing its bottom red bead, giving her an off-kilter look, and I found myself listing to the side as I regarded her. As I gazed into dark, round eyes rimmed with think black eyeliner, I gulped. I was looking at a child, twelve at most, maybe much younger. Bud's fifth grader looked older than this sad little bird.

"Miss Steele?" She spoke tentatively, voice husky.

I nodded, thinking, at least she can read. My office door has my name emblazoned in stick-on black and gold letters. Very classy.

"I'm sorry to be crashed here."

I shrugged. "No problem, happens all the time. Must've been a rough one last night, huh? Shouldn't you be in school or something?"

"Not today. Sometimes we go, but not today. I needed to see you and I snuck in before the guard locked up so I could catch you first thing."

She began fussing with her hair again, pulling at her skirt, smoothing out the jacket. Clearly nervous gestures, a way to occupy her tiny, shaking hands until I responded.

I smiled. "Well, you caught me. Come on in."

I didn't have a good feeling about this, but what could I do? Besides, my solemn routine had been broken now, so what the hell?

CHAPTER 3

My office has two small rooms, no bathroom. The bathroom's down the hall and pretty grungy. About once a month, I scrub it out, as building cleaning service is practically nonexistent. Every couple of months I work on the plumbing. My fellow tenants don't seem to care about maintenance, but then, I've never set foot in the men's room, and never intend to.

My outer office has a couch, or guest bed, as some would call it, super comfy if you ignore the moths that fly out of the holes in the arms. I keep a woven basket of old magazines, mostly donated by Bud. As a waiting room, it needs work, but I rarely have clients waiting. There's also a small refrigerator, the table beside it holding a coffee maker, electric tea kettle, and a few assorted canisters filled with sugar, coffee and tea bags.

My inner office has two tall windows that look out over the parking lots and rows of mills beyond. In its heyday, the city had over a hundred granite mills dotted along the river. It's an incredible view. In the morning the sun streams in and the office is warm and comfortable, not so much in the late afternoon. I have a huge oak partners desk that I discovered in one of the yet-to-be-renovated spaces. The landlord sold it to me for ten dollars and Bud helped me drag it down the hall. After I cleaned it up, polished the wood and fixed a couple of broken drawers, it gleamed. Sitting behind it makes me feel established and solid, as if my business had a long, illustrious history.

A four drawer file cabinet, three chairs, a gray metal locker, and two steamship prints on the wall complete my décor. I store valuables and my camera equipment in the locker, but any two-bit crook could pop the lock in three seconds. I wasn't sure I should offer coffee to my visitor. Didn't it stunt growth or something? Instead I invited her in and she took the most comfy chair. I sat in my swivel chair, and scooted it around the desk to sit beside her.

"So, what's up?"

"I'm sorry to bother you so early in the morning, but Mrs. Silva said you could help me and I really need help."

Ebbie Silva, a friend of a friend, had hired me a few months earlier to track down her brother-in-law. He had skipped out on her sister and Ebbie wanted a word with him. A few quick phone calls and I managed to dredge him up. When I handed Ebbie his address, I almost felt sorry for the guy.

"How is Ebbie?"

She shrugged and fidgeted. "Don't know her too well. Lives near us, that's all. She told me you can find people. I need you to find someone for me."

"Oh?"

"My friend, she's gone missing."

"What did you say your name was?"

Her face reddened and she gave me a shy, kid's smile. "Oh, sorry, it's Natalie, Natalie Remy. I been so stressed about Lisa. That's who I'm lookin' for, my friend, Lisa. I so worried, I'm kinda out of it, you know? It's just she's been gone for a couple of days and I'm getting freaked."

She was trembling now, rubbing her hands together. I caught a glimpse of an incredibly thin arm inside her coat sleeve. I knew with certainty I was way out of my depth.

"Hey, are you hungry? I think better with food and a cup of tea."

"Well, I—"

I rose, smiling down at her. "My treat. I'll put it on my expense account. Come on, Dino's is right around the corner. We can talk while we eat."

She followed me out of the office and down the stairs, her heels clattering at every step. The buildings and lots along Quarry Street were quiet as we walked side by side, maintaining the silence except for the drum beat of Natalie's high heels. She hovered close, occasionally brushing against me the way good friends do as they walk and talk. This was a needy child. Where was her mother?